THE PAST TENSE

OF LOVE

THE PAST TENSE OF LOVE

ELIZABETH CADELL

G.K. Hall & Co.   •   Chivers Press
Thorndike, Maine USA   Bath, England

LARGE
PRINT
FIC
Cade
C1

This Large Print edition is published by G.K. Hall & Co., USA
and by Chivers Press, England.

Published in 1999 in the U.S. by arrangement with
Brandt & Brandt Literary Agents, Inc.

Published in 1999 in the U.K. by arrangement with
Raymond Reynolds and Caroline Cadell.

U.S. Hardcover 0-7838-8593-8 (Romance Series Edition)
U.K. Hardcover 0-7540-3771-1 (Chivers Large Print)
U.K. Softcover 0-7540-3772-X (Camden Large Print)

The text of this Large Print edition is unabridged.
Other aspects of the book may vary from the original edition.

Set in 16 pt. Plantin by Minnie B. Raven.

Printed in the United States on permanent paper.

British Library Cataloguing in Publication Data available

Library of Congress Catalog Number: 99-94107
ISBN 0-7838-8593-8 (lg. print : hc : alk. paper)

THE PAST TENSE
OF LOVE

Chapter One

The packages lying on the floor of the narrow hall were difficult to sort. Not only were they of unidentifiable shape and size, but they had been bought in the same department store and were in uniform green-and-white wrapping paper.

"That one's mine," Aunt Elvira said, after prodding it. "And this . . . No, that's not. It's yours, Dale." She turned to regard, frowning, the forms of the two young women lounging on the sofa. "Come along, come along," she urged briskly. "Kerry, get up; your sister and I have to be off. It's almost five o'clock. Dale, did you buy these cotton vests, or did I?"

"You did." Dale yawned, stretched and got reluctantly to her feet. "Heavens, I'm tired!"

"You can rest when you get home. Come and sort your parcels and then we can get away and catch the early train. Look" — she pointed — "these must be the dusters you bought."

Kerry, still lying with eyes half-closed, spoke lazily.

"I've told you that I'll be home before you will. Why not leave the parcels for me to take? The car's large enough, heaven knows."

"A man who drives you down to the country for the weekend," her aunt stated, "doesn't want

7

to be cluttered up with your sister's underwear or your brother-in-law's bedroom slippers. Dale, where do you think that length of . . . Oh, this'll be it. Kerry, how can you live in such a poky little place?"

"Poky little place — London?"

"You know quite well what I mean. This flat. You earn a splendid salary and you could afford something better."

"Not in this district."

"They wouldn't get me to live in London" — Aunt Elvira gazed out disparagingly at the rows of chimney pots — "however much they paid me. How you keep your skin so clear through those winter fogs, I can't think."

"Nightly care and attention," Kerry murmured. "Elvira, relax."

"Don't call me Elvira, and for goodness' sake get up and clear away those tea things; they're in the way. Dale, this big parcel must be your dress."

"Dress?" Kerry's eyes opened and apprehension looked out of them. "Dress?"

"A nice new dress for Dale. Want to see it?"

Kerry shuddered.

"No. Dale, haven't I begged and begged you not to let your out-of-date aunts choose your —"

"I am not out of date," Aunt Elvira declared, "and neither are your aunts Sylvia or Dulcie or Thea. Has Dale's husband ever complained about her dresses?"

"He's still seeing through them. When they've

been married a bit longer —"

"Get up and stop arguing," Dale broke in mildly. "It's a nice dress and George'll love it. Aunt Elvira, did you pay for these socks, or did I?"

Kerry, watching them, thought it not surprising that they were invariably taken for mother and daughter. It was interesting to study them as they were now, the two of them, away from the others. Dale, she knew — for the aunts were constantly saying so — was the very image of her mother as she had looked when they last saw her; it was therefore reasonable to assume that today her mother would look something like Aunt Elvira. But perhaps not; there was a considerable difference in age. How many years?

She inquired, and saw her aunt stiffen with surprise.

"Well!" Her amazed glance came to rest on Kerry. "What an extraordinary thing to ask all of a sudden! Whatever put your mother into your head?"

"You. How old would she be?"

"Let me think. I'm the eldest and I'm sixty-six, and if you count downward there's Sylvia, sixty-four; Dulcie, sixty-two, and Thea, sixty. Then there was that big gap of fifteen years. Fifteen taken away from sixty leaves . . . leaves . . ."

"Forty-five. If she's still alive."

"There's no reason to suppose she isn't," Aunt Elvira said. "She was certainly alive five years ago, when she paid your last school bills. All of us

9

girls took after your grandfather, and he lived until he was nearly ninety. The Mostyns usually live until they're well into their eighties, and we're all thoroughgoing Mostyns."

True enough, Kerry mused. Mostyns all. In spite of Elvira and Dale's changes of name on marriage, Mostyns still. Placid, limited, undemanding, without curiosity or malice, totally unconcerned with world trends, totally uninterested in current affairs. Accustomed to existing on meager incomes. Self-contained. Ill educated. Completely contented with their narrow, uneventful lives. And entirely free from self-consciousness. Look at Aunt Elvira: shapeless woollen dress, marching boots and a jumble-sale hat, below which stringy strands of hair were hanging. Even Dale, she thought, turning her eyes on her sister, even the fair, beautiful Dale, who might have got herself out of the Mostyn stream, had on leaving school flowed straight back into it, married the first man who asked her, was already heavily pregnant but so much a Mostyn that among all the parcels lying about there was not one which contained the baby clothes she would need before long. When the pains came on, Kerry knew, she would call to mind overlooked items such as a crib or a carriage or a dozen or so diapers. Mostyns all. Except herself — and, presumably, her mother, who at the age of eighteen had performed the un-Mostyn-like act of leaving home and vanishing without trace.

She heard her aunt's voice.

"Kerry, wake up, will you? You haven't paid any attention to what I've been saying. When you get home, tell your Aunt Thea that I couldn't get the *vol-au-vent* pastry. She'll have to make it."

"God forbid," Dale and Kerry said in unison.

"Well, don't forget to tell her. She's depending on it. What's the name of this man you're taking down?"

"Nigel Frame."

"Didn't you say he's a writer of some sort?"

"I said he's a writer."

"Then I hope he isn't going to be like that other writer you took down last year — the one who ran over poor Thea's plants."

"That was the accountant," Dale corrected. "The writer was the one who walked out of church in the middle of the sermon."

"Now *that* was extraordinary, if you like," Aunt Elvira said indignantly.

"Not as extraordinary as the fact that he went in," Kerry said. She rose and raised her arms in a slow, luxurious stretch. "It's been fun. This is the first Friday I've had off for — oh, I can't remember."

"Have you heard how Lord Hazing is?" Dale asked.

"I rang up. He'll live, unfortunately."

"What was it he injured?" Aunt Elvira inquired.

"Small bone in his ankle," Kerry answered. "They put it in plaster — that's why I rang up to tell you I'd be free today. But I bet he'll be back in the office on Monday, even if he has to be carried. His temper'll be even more ghastly after this."

"How you can work for these bad-tempered brutes beats me," Aunt Elvira told her. "I can't believe this one's as bad as he sounds."

"He's worse."

"Then why —"

"You know why. Because if I work for these bad-tempered brutes, I can name my own salary. This is the third time the agency's put me into a job that a dozen other secretaries have walked out of. They know I'll stick it — as long as I want to."

"Is it really worth it?" Dale asked doubtfully.

"Of course it's worth it."

Worth it? How long would it have taken her otherwise, Kerry wondered, to get the enormous salary she was earning? How else could she have paid for this flat — small, but central? How could she have paid for the clothes she wore? Her employers — Lord Hazing was the third and in many ways the worst — could roar as loudly as they pleased; she had schooled herself to appear unmoved. Worth it? Yes. Especially as men of this type were too busy making millions to have time to spare to seduce their secretaries. Surliness was easier to cope with than sexiness. Yes, anything was worth it, just so long as there was, at every month's end, that wonderful, all-rewarding check.

"Myself," Aunt Elvira commented, "I think

you'd be a lot happier at home, helping your aunts."

This remark brought peals of laughter from her nieces; incensed, she left them to their amusement and went into the bedroom to prepare herself for the journey home. Dale, recovering, addressed Kerry.

"It's a long time since you took one of your men friends home," she commented. "Is this a serious affair?"

"I wouldn't say so."

"Then why raise their hopes? The aunts', I mean — not the men's. You've got them all steamed up. Aunt Elvira didn't only buy a dress for me, she bought one for herself. And they've been cooking for the past three days — cakes, pies and some pretty awful puddings."

"Oh God," groaned Kerry. "Just like last year."

"Yes. And then it comes to nothing, and they think it's because they did something wrong. Couldn't you marry this one, for a change?"

"I might. But I doubt if I will."

"What's he like?"

"Married at thirty, divorced his wife at thirty-three, is now thirty-six and hasn't wasted the intervening years."

"You don't sound in love," Dale commented.

But even if Kerry were, how would anybody know? she wondered. Nobody had ever got anything out of Kerry, and since she had come to live in London, five years ago, she had grown more and more enigmatic. The old friendliness, the old sympathies were still there, but the careless, carefree Kerry had merged gradually into this cool, poised, sophisticated semistranger. She visited her aunts now and then, but her real life was here in this flat, with its bare, austere, immaculate look, its very orderliness a proof of the distance Kerry had put between herself and her cluttered, disorganized home.

Dale studied her as she cleared the teacups onto a tray. No two sisters, she thought, could ever have been less alike; only their mother's assurance on her sole, brief reappearance twenty years ago could have made them believe that they had not had different fathers. She, Dale, blond, blue-eyed, said to be her mother's very image; and Kerry, dark-haired, with eyes that could look gray or green, with a firm mouth and chin. Not pretty in the conventional sense, but something more, something that Dale's husband George had once called effortless allure. Heads might not turn in the street, but once a man had time to look at her, he was — George again — hooked.

"This man Nigel Frame," she resumed. "Did you tell him about our erring mother?"

"Yes. I always do tell a man when he begins to get serious, in the hope of cooling him off. Unfortunately, they all take it in their stride. You'd think illegitimacy was a mere talking point."

"That," Aunt Elvira said with displeasure from the doorway, "is not a word I like to hear you use."

"You know a nicer one?" Kerry smiled.

"I have always," Aunt Elvira answered obliquely, "discussed your mother freely with you both. So have your other aunts. All we have ever asked is that you girls should retain your respect and affection for her."

"We do, we do, oh, we do," Kerry assured her, edging round her with the laden tray. "We'd retain our respect and affection for our father, too, if only she'd stopped long enough to say who he was. Wait a minute and I'll help you on with your coat."

"I don't want . . . Good heavens, Kerry" — Aunt Elvira turned to stare into the kitchen — "you're surely not going to worry about putting those few fiddling little things into the dishwasher are you?"

"I'm not going to worry; I'm just going to put them in."

Aunt Elvira, opening her mouth to complain of her niece's tone, closed it again; the tone, after all, had been mild enough. It was the undertone that always baffled her, and baffled her sisters.

"If you don't like your home," she said, pursuing her rather wavering line of thought, "why do you bother to bring these young men down to it?"

"To fill in the background." Kerry took her aunt's coat and held it out. "Thank you for coming up. I've enjoyed it."

"So've I, but it was expensive, all that shopping," Aunt Elvira said. "I don't know what

Thea's going to say when she hears what I had to pay for the gardening gloves." She sighed. "They'll all be tired, I expect. They always are, preparing for one of your visits. And somebody's been after them, been after us all for signatures to appeal for a bigger church, but George said it's no use talking about the increase in the local population, or pointing out that there are fifty thousand in High Green where once there were only fifty. If the extra forty-nine or so thousand don't go to church, which George says they don't, where's the need for a bigger one?"

"The vicar thinks that if the church is bigger, they'll come," Dale explained.

"Quite so. And if you don't agree with him," Aunt Elvira said, "Then you send his spirits right down into his boots, poor man. Come along, Dale. Goodbye, Kerry. Thank you for the tea."

Kerry took them down in the lift, saw them into a taxi and stood watching them drive away; then she went back to the flat and packed a suitcase and assembled the food and drink she always took with her on her visits to her aunts. When Nigel Frame rang the doorbell, she was ready to leave.

He drove slowly through the crowded streets, and she leaned against the soft leather cushions and admired the car's gleaming fittings. All this, she mused, and the driver too. If she wanted them.

"Well?" he asked after a time. "How'm I doing in that survey you're making?"

16

"So-so. Why don't you go after a blond? You and I are too dark to go well together."

"My wife was a blond. We didn't go well together."

She glanced at him. He looked older than his years, fit, clever and comfortably off. He was good-looking and, in certain moods, amusing, and he had succeeded in holding her attention longer than any other man had done.

This success he owed to the fact that he shared her taste for sport. He had thought, on their first meeting, that she was interested only as a spectator, but he had learned that if he wanted to see her after office hours, if he wanted to develop the affair so promisingly begun, he would have to exert himself — not, as with the women he had hitherto pursued, on dance floors or in night clubs, but on tennis courts and ice rinks, in swimming pools and on horseback. She was good at all these forms of exercise, but she wanted to be better. Her working hours were erratic, since she worked for employers who paid her to be available whenever she was needed, but once she was free, she went straight to the Sports Club, to which she belonged. If a man wanted to enjoy her company, he could enjoy it there. Intimate little dinners — Nigel Frame's specialty — were out. Other intimacies were also out, for he had found that after a busy day in the office and a strenuous evening thrashing up and down a pool in near-championship free-style, all her passion was spent and all a man could do was drive the husk home and have the door shut in his face.

It was not his idea of an ideal siege. Even the sex angle was acute, since her interpretation of the current freedoms was that a girl could yes or no, just as she pleased. So far, he had had a series of careless, casual, unemphatic but nevertheless unyielding nos, and was beginning to marvel at his stamina; the only progress he had made in seven months was in swimming and serving aces.

"How many aunts are we going to visit?" he inquired.

"Four. One widowed, three maiden. In descending order, Elvira, Sylvia, Dulcie and Thea. Aunt Elvira married the last-but-two vicar and lived for a time at the vicarage, but the others have never left Orchard House."

"Which is where you and your sister were brought up."

"Yes. Except that, unlike my aunts, we went away to school. They didn't. They were educated, if you can call it educated, by my grandfather."

"Are we carting all this drink down for them?"

"No. You. They don't keep any. They'll put the bottles out and we'll help ourselves and they'll try not to make remarks about this generation's extraordinary need for stimulants. They don't like heavy meals, so if the dinner tonight doesn't fill you, you can order sandwiches when you go back to your room at the pub. And if you can't bring yourself to go to church on Sunday, pretend you're some other religion."

18

"Buddhist? Moslem?"

"Either or both. And remember to leap to your feet every time they come into or go out of a room. Remember to open doors for them and remember to push their chairs in at meals."

"What — all four?"

"One at a time. And if they ask you what kind of books you write, skate around it and say you're a historian. And don't say *bloody* or worse."

"You mean you stuck this until you were eighteen?"

"I like my aunts. If you're offered a second helping at meals, don't take it, because there isn't one."

"Then how can I —"

"It'll be offered. They'll ask if you'd like to have a little more of this or that. Say no, thank you, it was delicious but you couldn't. And there's only one bathroom, so if you hear anybody going near it, keep away because it embarrasses them to meet strangers going or coming."

"How shall I ever be able to tear myself away?"

"I warned you."

"You weren't specific enough. Couldn't we spend the weekend somewhere else? Or is this another of the hurdles a man has to heave himself over in his pursuit of you?"

"You insisted on coming."

"I thought a couple of quiet days in a country garden would calm my nerves. I thought I might even get you to lie on a hammock with me and

19

. . . well, swing. I wish to God I knew why I wanted to marry you."

"You told me why. I'm your ideal of —"

"Yes, yes, yes. All that. The exasperating thing about you is that you don't look the athletic type. A man, meeting you, thinks that he's soon going to get his arms round a soft, silky, yielding, beautiful body. Then what? He finds himself shivering on the edge of a swimming bath or pool with a stopwatch in his hand. Or he tries to impress you by diving off the top board and practically rips his inside open. Or he goes trit-trot-trit-trot on a bloody horse and scrapes the skin off his outside. I must have banged my head on the bottom when I did that first high dive, or maybe I'm just naturally crazy. Can't you give up sport and think up some other way of letting off steam?"

She said nothing. She knew that his summary of a man's problems in getting to know her was fair enough. What he didn't know, she mused, was that when she had first come to live in London, she had been as willing as any other girl to accept invitations to dance or dine, until she realized that she had chosen to work for the type of employer who did not feel bound to keep any engagement his secretary might make. Constantly breaking dates had been a wearing process, and not conducive to popularity. So it was easier, healthier and in the long run more fun to take a taxi to the Sports Club, which had both indoor and outdoor facilities and a bar at which she could order sandwiches before going home to bed.

"When are you going to take a holiday?" Nigel inquired. "You're due for one, aren't you? How about now, before Hazing gets on to his two feet again?"

"I might suggest it."

"If you could get a few days off, would you do a trip with me in Switzerland? Don't say yes or no yet; think about it. The car's comfortable, and early June's a nice time of year — roads not too crowded with stinking tourists. I'll look up hotels with no tennis courts and no swimming pools, and then perhaps I can make some headway. Will you think it over?"

She hesitated. She had seen it coming, and now here it was; she would have to decide how she was going to respond, if she was going to respond. Why hesitate? She liked him more than any other man she had met. If she wanted to marry — and what woman didn't? — she could hardly find anyone likely to suit her better. She wanted a home and children, so why go on with a difficult job with a fiendish-tempered boss and long, uncertain hours?

It was a pity, she thought with a touch of regret, that the offer had not been confined to a Swiss tour. She wanted to travel, not as she travelled with her employers, long, tiring journeys by air, with no time or leisure to see anything of the places she went to. She had never crossed the English Channel. She had never been on a leisurely trip in a car. She longed to see France and Italy and Spain. So why not go with this man?

"All right. I'll think about it," she said.

"That's something. Will it really be your first trip to the Continent?"

"Yes. Dale and I arranged to go once, and then she got married."

"Well, we'll get married. I, Nigel Norman Frame, take thee, Catherine Cromer to Switzerland as a preliminary. Incidentally, as your aunts are called Mostyn, where does the Cromer come from? Is he the chap your mother didn't marry?"

"No. It was the name of the vicar my aunt Elvira married. He thought it would be a good idea to adopt us, so we took his name, but for some reason the adoption idea was dropped, and Dale and I never went to live at the vicarage. We stayed with my other aunts at Orchard House. When Aunt Elvira's husband died, she came back to it."

"Tell me those names again, will you?"

She told him. "And my mother, if you're interested," she added, "was called Madeleine."

Thirty years ago, Orchard House — a large, square, solid building with a two-acre, untended garden — had been surrounded on three sides by green fields and on the fourth by endless stretches of orchard. In spring, the beauty of the blossoms attracted so many sightseers that the four older Mostyn girls had once put before their father a scheme for setting up a table at their gate and selling the pictures that one of them, Sylvia, had painted of the scene. This plan old Mr. Mostyn vetoed on the grounds that it might expose them to undue notice from strangers, and although this seemed to them highly desirable from a vendor's point of view, they did not question his decision. Father knew best, and even if on occasion he didn't, none of them would have dreamed of telling him so, for as well as being wise, he was old and frail and had never recovered from the shock of being widowed. His wife, more than thirty years his junior, had died in childbirth producing, after an interval of fifteen years, a fifth daughter.

The Mostyn world was small. It could be said to be little more than two and a half acres in extent, for beyond the high, encircling garden wall was nothing but the little hamlet of High Green, which contained a tiny church, a vast vicarage, a smithy, four cottages grouped around a duck pond, and a ruined flour mill in which the little Mostyn girls sometimes played. Leading to this peaceful cluster were footpaths that meandered between meadows and streams. The neighbouring towns, three miles away on either side, might have been in another country, so little did they affect the lives of the Mostyns. Their food grew or grazed nearby. Water bubbled in brooks or gushed from pumps. The girls' education was taken in hand by the scholarly Mr. Mostyn, a stooping, gentle figure they seldom saw outside his dim, book-lined study. A housekeeper named Mrs. Pierce sewed strong, sensible garments for

Elvira, and these passed in due course to Sylvia and then to Dulcie and finally to Thea. In times of sickness, somebody bicycled out to the telephone kiosk at the crossroads and summoned old Doctor Coxton, who bumped out in his high-slung Ford and brought into the house a strange, unaccustomed flavour of masculinity.

While Mrs. Mostyn was alive, and maids easy to obtain, no household duties devolved on the four girls. Despite this, they led very busy lives. Their studies took up very little of their time, for old Mr. Mostyn's method was simply to outline the course of study to be pursued by the intelligent and diligent pupil: this plan, so successfully applied in the past to himself, produced no results whatever from his daughters, who were only moderately intelligent and not at all studious, and whose diligence was applied to more absorbing pursuits. Elvira went in for embroidery, using the large dining table to trace designs and scattering pins that found their way into the pies or the porridge. Sylvia, a Teach-Yourself-To-Play propped on the music stand, thumped for hours on the ancient piano in the drawing room or, with camp stool and easel, sat painting in the orchards. Dulcie had at a very early age discovered in the attics a stock of dusty cardboard boxes into which had been thrown the stamp collections of her father and grandfather; these she sorted tirelessly and stuck into albums. Thea's passion was for herb-growing and cactus plants; anybody wishing to find her in the house

24

had only to follow the trail of muddy footprints.

But that was in the green, pastoral past, before enemy bombs had uprooted the fruit trees and flattened the cottages, before the adjacent towns had sent out lines of cement soldiers to occupy the green vacant spaces and to insure that nothing ever grew there again, before the little church was surrounded and shut in, its spire alone visible above the new slate roofs, looking like a missile awaiting the countdown. Today, Orchard House, its garden a green oasis, looked out on a desert of bungalows with foreign names and integrated garages.

Some changes had also taken place within the house. Old Mr. Mostyn was dead. The servants had vanished, never to be replaced. A new vicar had been appointed and a new doctor had set up his plate near by. And Madeleine, the youngest Miss Mostyn, had left home on a windy autumn day, taking a minimum of luggage and leaving no address. Her sisters were still trying to find reasons for this shattering event when the vicar shattered them even more by proposing to Elvira.

There was a considerable delay before the marriage took place, as the vicar was unable to dislodge his mother and sisters and sisters' husbands from the vicarage, to which they had come uninvited and in which they had taken up free quarters. During this interval, there came out of the blue a letter to Elvira from Madeleine, asking if they could meet, and giving an address in

25

London. Elvira went up charged with affectionate messages from her sisters and returned with two little girls aged three and two respectively. Their mother, having entrusted them to the care of their aunts, disappeared once more.

The two children merged happily into the life at Orchard House — so happily, that for many years the visits of the postman were dreaded, lest another letter should come from Madeleine, this time asking for her children to be returned. But no letter came. Elvira married and moved to the vicarage; returning to Orchard House on the death of her husband two years later, she fortunately brought with her a substantial legacy, which was used to close the gap between rising prices and the Mostyn sisters' unexpanding income.

Today, Dale was married to the grandson of old Doctor Coxton and lived in a small red villa half a mile away. At Orchard House, Elvira cooked, Sylvia made beds and dusted, Dulcie ironed and Thea grew vegetables — but between the performance of these household tasks, they continued to pursue their hobbies. Elvira still embroidered, Sylvia thumped the piano with the vigour she applied to punching pillows; Dulcie filled more and more stamp albums and Thea's pots of cactus plants grew more numerous. Accustomed all their lives to solitude, they viewed with astonishment the surrounding fever of bridge or bingo or cocktail or dinner parties, balls and barbecues, but felt no desire to join them. If they had needed companionship, they could have sought it within the home. But the four sisters lived separate lives, as they had done since childhood, meeting daily, but not merging, like ants, scurrying here and there, colliding, disengaging and going on their way. Dale and her husband, the new vicar and his wife, and Kerry and the friends she brought down — these were the only visitors to whom hospitality was extended. For Kerry's visits, her aunts united in an effort to provide fitting entertainment.

And on this occasion, as on previous occasions, things were not going well. Overeagerness had curdled the mayonnaise. The last two batches of buns were stodgy. The fish — surely it had been fresh?

"I tell you what; we'll make a curry sauce for it," Thea said. "I always think a curry sauce —"

"This is the fourth man she's brought down," Sylvia remarked, reaching for the onions. "I wish she'd settle on someone."

"Fifth," corrected Dulcie, who was polishing glasses.

"There was the one with red hair, and the shy one, and the one that broke the Wedgwood plate and the one who ran over the plants, and now this one. Five."

"They must think it rather peculiar, at the pub, I mean?" Thea said. "One after the other, and no sign of Kerry getting engaged. Sylvia, are you sure the *vol-au-vent* pastry was on Elvira's shopping list?"

"Certain. I wrote it on myself. Dulcie, did you remember to put sugar in the cake?"

"Yes. I measured it in that cup."

Sylvia licked a finger, laid it on the bottom of the cup and then licked it again.

"Salt," she pronounced. "It's not your fault. Elvira got the packets mixed up. You'd better go and get those glasses ready in the drawing room. Isn't it odd that they don't seem able to exist even for one short weekend without ruining their insides with all these drinks? Don't try to pour them out, as you did last time. You made rather a hash, if you remember."

"I was upset, that's why. You didn't see the way that young man lounged in a chair with his legs stretched out, and not so much as a word of apology when I tripped over them."

"Well, this time, leave them to do it all themselves."

They went upstairs later and changed their dresses and came down looking almost elegant, for although Elvira still gave them secondhand garments, they were no longer those she had worn; they came from parcels sent to the vicarage for distribution, from an organization known as Aid to Indigent Relatives of the Clergy. The A.I.R.C., Elvira's husband had pointed out the first time he came upon her skimming the cream, had other recipients in mind, but Elvira had replied that her sisters were related to him, and were far from rich. The supply might have ceased on the appointment of subsequent vicars, but Elvira had prudently retained the list of Indigent Relatives and had agreed to go on making the distribution.

The sisters were assembled in the drawing room, rather at a loss without Elvira, who had never before been absent and unable to take her place at the head of the reception committee. But even without her they made a handsome trio, having retained a large measure of the good looks they had had as girls. Sylvia was tall and drooping, Dulcie dumpy and Thea square and solid, but they all had dignity, and a manner unaffected and natural. Now they looked expectant: Kerry was coming, and with her not only the fifth man in the past two years, but also a rare touch of excitement and the only sophistication that ever entered their lives. Like sun-lovers, they prepared to make the most of the bright spell, storing up warmth against the long interval before her next visit. They loved Dale, but both Dale and her husband were part of them. Kerry was not, and never had been. She was warm and affectionate, but she was also detached and independent and they had never really known her. She must take after her father — but then again, perhaps not; had they ever really known her mother? Who would have dreamed that for all those years, when she had seemed so happy and so settled, she had been longing, so she told Elvira in London, to escape. Escape!

The weekend proved one of Kerry's most successful visits. Perhaps it was the man she brought this time, more friendly than the others, easier to talk to, with no eccentricities of dress or behaviour. Perhaps it was because they brought down so much food that there was no need to serve the fish with the curry sauce, or the blancmange, which had failed to set. The only unfortunate incident occurred when Thea chilled the red wine and *chambréed* the white, but even this could not spoil the success of the three days. It was almost, they said to each other long afterward, as though they had known what was to come. Sylvia was to say that she didn't want to claim psychic powers, but she had felt, all through Saturday and Sunday, that something was, so to speak, looming. She had *known*.

But she couldn't have known, Thea pointed out. How could she have known, when even Kerry didn't know?

Chapter Two

If the weekend had been, as Nigel Frame suspected, an experiment on Kerry's part to find out how much he could stand, she admitted to herself as they drove back to London on Sunday evening that he had passed the test creditably. But the admission, which should have reassured her, had the opposite effect; she slept badly and woke on Monday morning with the uneasy feeling that things were moving too fast for her liking.

But if she couldn't find anything wrong with him and was still feeling undecided, there must be something wrong with herself. She was spoiled, she decided. She enjoyed a man's freedom, a man's salary, a man's complete independence. She was not so much a girl hesitating on the brink of marriage as a bachelor reluctant to abandon his single status.

She turned off the gas and carried the coffee pot to the table. Yes, spoiled; that was it, she mused, depression overtaking her. She had grown selfish. If she didn't marry Nigel Frame, she would turn into one of those high-gloss career women who grew rich and smart and had brief, brisk, well-managed love affairs and became godmothers to other people's children. It was not what she wanted from life. But neither was the alternative — settling down with Nigel Frame.

Monday morning, she told herself finally, was not the time for brooding on life. She poured out some coffee, raised the cup to her lips and then put it down to answer the telephone. She had little doubt as to whose voice she would hear when she picked up the receiver; these dawn alerts were invariably blown from the same bugle.

"Miss Cromer?"

So. She had known that it would take more than a damaged ankle to keep him off the job. Next time, with luck, it might be his skull.

"Good morning, Lord Hazing. I hope you're feeling —"

"Don't go to the office. I want you down here."

"Very well. What time?"

"Now. I've told the office to send a car for you."

"Do you want any particular files?"

"If I'd wanted any particular files, I would have said so."

Crash. End of courteous instructions from employer to employee. Kerry pulled a face, drank her coffee and changed into a more informal dress. The last time she had been down to the Surrey mansion, she recalled, was to arrange a reception for a Swiss industrialist, and the time before that to assist the last Lady Hazing to draw up an inventory of her possessions on the eve of her departure to Bermuda with, she told Kerry, a man who could open his mouth without barking.

The marriage — Lord Hazing's second — had not lasted long; Kerry had expected him to try again, but the months had gone by and he had remained wifeless, though not womanless.

The car arrived before she had finished changing. When she was ready, she went down and greeted the chauffeur.

"Good morning, Gatesley."

" 'Morning, Miss Cromer." He paused before closing the car door. "No luggage?"

"No instructions about luggage," she told him. "This must be just to find out what his lordship wants me to do in the office."

"From what I heard, miss, he's to keep that foot off the ground for a week. Not that he will. All the same, I'd have thought he'd want you to stay at the house."

"That's not what he said."

"Then it's not what he wants. Fast or slow, miss?"

"Nice and slow, with a stop for coffee. I'll say we had a flat."

She enjoyed the drive and felt entitled to prolong it; she was not looking forward to her arrival. A man who was a terror when fit would be a very devil with his ankle in plaster.

When she was ushered into his presence, she saw that her surmise had been correct; all he lacked was horns and a tail. His face, dark and distorted with anger, glared at her across a disordered bed and an out-thrust, bandaged foot.

"What the hell kept you?" he demanded.

"Slight engine trouble."

She expected him to point out the truth: that no car driven by Gatesley ever had engine trouble. Instead, he turned to grope among the collection of articles on the bedside table.

"I hope you're feeling better," she said.

"Let's cut out the courtesies. Take this collection of cards and acknowledge them, and get rid of the flowers and the fruit any damned way you please. And see that no more clutter of this sort is sent down from the office."

The machine-gun rattle of orders was no more than normal, but his tone held a suppressed fury that she felt could not be attributed to the temporary check imposed by his accident. She was not surprised at his next words.

"There's something else. I'd made arrangements to go to France. I've had to change my plans."

So that was it. It wasn't the interruption to his work that was burning him up. He had made arrangements to go to France several times in the past month; it was merely his way of informing her that he would be away from the office for a day or two pursuing a woman who interested him, and that she was to remain glued to her office chair until he returned to take the reins. But he couldn't go limping to a new love, and so it would be interesting to learn how he proposed to deal with the situation.

To her surprise, he took up a book and held it out.

"Here. Take this," he ordered.

She took it. It was one of the specially bound copies of Nigel Frame's last book that she had bought at great expense last Christmas and presented to her employer; his sole acknowledgment had been a surly sentence to the effect that she had wasted her money.

"Pay close attention," he commanded. "This is important, and I don't want to have to say it more than once. I was on the point of going to France, but this bloody ankle has finished that. I've decided to send you instead."

"I see."

She saw nothing save the fact that this time the trip was a genuine one. But she would have maintained her calm demeanour if he had announced that she was to set off without delay to Afghanistan.

"You'll take that book with you. You won't let it out of your sight at anytime — *any* time, d'you understand? — throughout the journey. Don't pack it. Put it with a couple of others into your flight bag, to look like reading matter for the trip. This" — he took from the table and handed her a long, unsealed envelope — "is the address you're going to. You leave at eight-thirty tomorrow morning. I've instructed the office to transfer the tickets to your name. You'll fly to Paris and from there you'll fly to Nantes, and after Nantes you'll have a short train journey. These" — he handed her another envelope — "are the tickets. Do you speak French?"

"Not well."

"God knows what passes for education these days. Well, you won't need much French for this job. I needn't add that this is an extremely important and highly confidential matter — a personal matter, in fact, entrusted to you only because I can't go myself. Explain that when you get there. When you've handed over the book, you can take your holiday. I shan't need you for a month. I'll expect you back in the office on July the fifth. That's all. If you've any questions, don't ask them."

He did not ask her whether her passport was in order; it was a matter that, travelling as they invariably did at short notice, she could never afford to neglect. He pressed a bell, and while she waited for a servant to show her out, she saw his eyes on her with the first look of personal interest she had ever seen in them, assessing her capacity, she thought, to execute these unusual orders. She gave him as cool and as frank a survey, reflecting that if someone in the past, one of those women of his, had taken strong measures when he began to get above himself, he would be a better man today. It was too late now, of course, but somebody could have stopped him from becoming the bully he was. Nobody should ever be allowed to ride roughshod. He was undeniably handsome, once one looked beyond the scowl; his mouth, when not twisted in a snarl, was well shaped, and his eyes, if not invariably screwed up in a glare, could have looked pleasant. He might even have looked more like those early photographs that his ex-wife had instructed her, in the process of packing up, to throw into the waste-paper basket. Looking at him now, she could see clearly the remnants of the charm that the camera had caught and recorded. A feeling of regret, almost of liking, stirred in her — and died as the servant appeared to show her out.

Lord Hazing's farewell was merely a nod. Holding the book and the envelopes, she went out to the car and for the first part of the journey back to London sat gazing out absently at the fitful sunshine, regretting that her first cross-Channel trip should be a mere hop-and-skip to Nantes. She could think of many other more exciting projects — the Golden Arrow to Paris, for example, and then a sleeper thundering through the night, and then a swaying restaurant car and delicious French food eaten in company with mesdames or preferably messieurs, and at last arrival at a golden beach with a blue dancing sea on one side and green waving palms on the other.

Sighing, she drew out the tickets. Flight to Paris. Flight to Nantes. Train to . . . She found it difficult to decipher the name: Gaston-le-Grand. Not a blood-stirring schedule; the only thing to be said for it was that it had compensating undertones of mystery. Why was she being dispatched so urgently, book clutched in hand? If this was another of his amorous adventures, didn't the woman have a telephone over which he could make his explanations or his excuses?

And if he had to send a book, why one that he had said was not worth reading? All that was certain was the importance of the errand; she knew that he had been as tense as a tight wire, humming with the need for speed, maddened by the accident that had prevented him from setting off himself.

It was no use guessing. She had her orders, and she would carry them out as usual.

She opened the envelopes. In one were the tickets to be changed. In the other, which she had expected to contain a card or a letter, there was merely a slip of paper with a name and address:

> Madame Daumier
> Maison du Bois
> Gaston-le-Grand

Puzzled, she picked up the book and shook open the pages. No message fell out, but inside the cover she saw scrawled in Lord Hazing's bold, picturesque but almost illegible hand, two lines:

This book contains something you refused to accept fifteen years ago. With love as always.

Fifteen years. That placed Madame Daumier between Lady Hazing One and Lady Hazing Two. Fifteen from sixty-two — he would have been forty-seven. And as he was uninterested in girls or even in young women, Madame Daumier must have been around forty, no doubt a sensible, experienced woman able to cope with his tantrums. What had she refused fifteen years ago? And what could she find in Nigel Frame's book? Highly unsuitable literature, one would have thought, for a woman now aged fifty-five, living in a house in a wood and probably out of touch with the latest modes in human misbehaviour.

She put speculation aside. She had little interest in Madame Daumier or in the relationship between her and Lord Hazing. He had had other women in the past; he would have other women in the future. If there was one word that summed him up better than any other, it was *virile*.

She turned her thoughts to her own affairs. Clothes? It would be as well to buy something really cool.

"Gatesley."

"Yes, miss?"

"Drop me at Barfontes, will you?"

He gave a long whistle, which indicated both awe and a caution to go easy. But he took her there. The remainder of the day was a tense, concentrated period during which she cleared up at the office, telephoned, paid a visit to the bank, packed and got in touch with Nigel Frame.

"Where did you say?" he asked her.

She had refused to go out to dinner and so he had settled, reluctantly, for omelettes at her flat. He was leaning against the door of the kitchen, drink in hand, watching her as she cooked them.

"I didn't say. It's somewhere near Nantes. I've got to deliver a book. One of your books, incidentally. The presentation copy I gave him last Christmas."

"And which he couldn't read. What's the matter with posting it?"

"This is a kind of personal thing, I gather."

"And afterward, what?"

"He's given me a month's holiday, but —"

"Good. We'll —"

"— but I want to spend most of it with Dale and George."

"George?"

"You met him. Dale's husband. They came in to drinks yesterday evening."

"Oh yes, George. George didn't take to me. Did you notice?"

"I noticed."

"What put him off? My literary reputation?"

"Your embroidered waistcoat."

"Too bad. If it's Nantes you're going to, I suggest we wash out Switzerland and do a tour of the Loire châteaux, if you know what I'm talking about."

"Certainly I know. We had a French mistress at school who came from Tours. You only had to mention the Loire and she forgot what she was meant to be teaching and got out her girlhood snaps. She — what are you looking for?"

"Mushrooms."

"None. If you can't bear your omelette plain,

I'll sprinkle some cheese onto it."

But he had found and was opening a jar of shrimps.

"I've got a godmother who lives at Tours," he said. "I'll pay her a surprise visit, and then I'll pick you up at Nantes. But you'll have to let me know where and when."

"I've no idea when. Write your godmother's name and address and phone number in my diary, and I'll get in touch with you."

He did not seek more detailed information. He had learned that in matters concerned with her work, she exercised a discretion that she said was due to her employer, but which he found excessive and irritating.

She sent him home early and dialed Dale's number, aware that their conversation would sound like a tape recording of similar exchanges they had had over the past few years.

"You don't mean you're going off on a trip with him?"

"Yes."

"Why? You've never gone off with anybody before. When I asked you if this was special, you said no, it wasn't, so why go away for a whole month and —"

"Two weeks. I'm saving the rest for you and George."

"George didn't like him. I wasn't going to tell you, but he said he thought he was serious about you — this Frame man, I mean — and that upset George."

"Shouldn't it have reassured him?"

"How could it reassure him if he didn't like him?"

"Can I come straight down to you when I get back?"

"Good heavens, why ask? You don't have to bring him with you, do you?"

"No. Well, goodbye for now. I'll see you —"

"Kerry, wait a minute."

"Well?"

"Look, you know I try not to interfere, but — well, aren't you being a bit precipitate? What I'm trying to say is that you're free to run your own life, but I'd just like you to make sure it's the right man before you do anything silly, that's all. George says —"

"You mean I can only have a preliminary canter if I'm quite sure I'm going to buy the horse?"

"You always try to get out of it by making jokes. All I wish is — Oh well, take care of yourself."

Smiling, Kerry put down the receiver in time to prevent Dale from reciting the last line, which was always an impassioned plea to keep herself inviolate until Fate turned up another prize like George.

When she went down early next morning and handed her suitcase to the waiting Gatesley, she was holding Nigel Frame's book. The chauffeur drove her to the airport, and when her luggage had passed into the airline's care, she went to the

42

book stall and lingered over the choice of reading matter for the journey. There was a shattering moment when, having paid for her purchases, she walked away and then discovered that she had put down for a moment and forgotten to pick up again the book that was the sole purpose of her travels. Cold with apprehension, she went back; to her relief, it was where she had left it. Picking it up, she saw that it had been resting on a pile of French phrase books, and bought one. Glancing through it on the plane, she thought most of the sentences well within her linguistic scope, and it was not until she was on the ground at Orly that she made the discovery that a phrase book was only one end of a conversation; the trick was to discover what was said in reply. Struggling to snatch recognizable phrases from the incomprehensible stream flowing around her, she told herself that she had been a fool to allow so thick a layer of rust to form over her schoolgirl French.

Orly couldn't be called Paris — but it was Paris all the same, and she was there. But not for long. There was another plane to catch. Misunderstanding the directions she was given, she found herself with a raging thirst and only a few moments in which to buy a long, cool drink. She hurried to the counter and was about to place her order when a black-frocked, black-hatted priest appeared beside her, commandeered the attention of the attendant and proceeded to make a leisurely choice between several brands of sweets. Kerry, chafing, eyed him with loathing and thought he had a face like a fox. By the time he had completed his purchase and counted out the money in coins of the smallest possible denomination, the flight number had been called and she was obliged to go without her drink.

She had long legs, and she used them to outdistance most of the other passengers on the approach to the aircraft. Boarding, she saw with satisfaction that she had managed to secure a window seat. She turned for a moment to free the strap of her handbag from the luggage of a passing passenger; when she had released it, she found to her fury that Fox-face had slipped past her and settled himself by the window.

She glanced to right and left. There were no other vacant window seats. There was nothing to do but take her place beside the priest and hope that the third seat in the row would remain vacant. At the last moment, however, it was claimed by a latecomer — a tall but extremely stout, extremely agitated old gentleman carrying three large books and a roll of newspapers. He removed his hat and placed it on the rack, revealing a few strands of gray hair that, however carefully they might have been arranged earlier over his otherwise bald head, now strayed in wispy confusion. He bent forward to push the newspapers into the rack in front of his seat; the books slipped from under his arm and fell into the aisle, while the newspapers unrolled themselves and fell onto Kerry's lap. A steward retrieved the books and a passenger on the other side of the aisle picked up the old gentleman's spectacles, which had fallen off. He was assisted into his seat and the safety belt adjusted around his protuberant middle. The plane's engines roared. The priest took a sweet from the packet he had bought, made the sign of the cross and fingered his rosary. Kerry hoped that his prayers would remain unanswered — and then, reflecting that they were probably for a safe flight, hoped they would receive priority. She settled back in her seat, unfastened her safety belt, opened a paperback and wished that she had remembered to buy a guide book that dealt with the Loire châteaux, for in spite of her claim to know a good deal about them, she in fact remembered nothing. It was disheartening to come across, almost daily, evidences of her limited education. For the granddaughters of a once-noted scholar, she mused, she and Dale had poor records. Dale had been pushed, resisting strongly, through successive classes at school until, arriving at Orchard House for the Christmas holidays just after her sixteenth birthday, she had announced that her education was completed and she would not, therefore, be returning to school the following term. She herself, Kerry acknowledged, had been an even greater fool, for she had learned easily, had done well and had every chance of entering a university. But she had elected, instead, to leave school, and had enrolled herself at a London

45

secretarial college with a view of getting a job and earning money as soon as possible. Money. She sighed. Money, money, money. Her mother had arranged payment for their school bills, but school was over and the aunts had no money to spare. Even the income Elvira had inherited and which once had seemed so large, now did no more than cover their living expenses. Money. With her first paycheck, she had felt a surge of relief and triumph: she was independent. But later there had come the realization that she had made the wrong decision. She had acted, as she had acted all her life, on her own initiative. Her aunts had never in their lives given her or Dale a word of advice, but who was to say it would have been heeded?

She was brought back to the present by a jet of ice-cold liquid which, splashing over from the glass that a steward had just handed to the stout old gentleman, caused her to give a yelp of surprise. Moaning penitently, he attempted to assist her in her mopping-up operations. She reached into her bag for another handkerchief and realized with dismay that the stream was sticky. The steward brought a towel, and the old gentleman continued to moan, offering apologies in a variety of languages.

"Mademoiselle, je vous demande pardon." He was almost weeping. He turned from her and pulled down the little tray in front of his seat and placed his glass on it; it tilted, the glass slid rapidly sideways and its contents flowed impartially

over his trousers and Kerry's stockings. This, to her relief, directed his attention to his own troubles, and she saw him attempting to fold himself over his still-fastened safety belt as he groped for his glasses, which had fallen off again. The wisps of hair fell across his eyes; his breath became alarmingly loud and laboured.

No help from the church, Kerry noted in disgust; all Fox-face had done was draw his skirts aside and open his breviary. If she had had a sticky drink handy, she would have poured it over him — but enveloped as he was in those thick black folds, she thought he would have been safe from either freezing or scalding.

The old gentleman was asking, in Swedish or Dutch or German, if she would forgive him. His voice was low and soft and came out as a kind of hoarse whisper that, combined with his earnest, intense stare, gave the impression that he was imparting secrets.

"Please don't worry," she told him. "I'll dry off in time."

"English? My dear young lady, I beg you to forgive my clumsiness." His English was fluent, but his accent was guttural, and he gave to some words a curiously rolling treatment that made them sound like tongue twisters. "Perhaps we could order from the attendant another little towel to —"

"No, thank you. It's not necessary."

But his distress was genuine, and he went on, miserable and ashamed, endeavouring to make amends. Her irritation rose until she was on the verge of an outburst, and then, as almost always at this point, she found herself laughing, and laughed more at the ludicrous expression of relief that overspread his face. He put on his glasses and peered at her. Might not this be hysteria? No. She was an angel, she had forgiven him. A smile trembled on his lips, widened; in a moment he was shaking violently and uttering wheezy gasps of laughter.

Well, this was life, she thought resignedly. To hear other girls describing their travels, you'd think there'd be a handsome young man on one side and a suave middle-aged charmer on the other, but all she'd drawn was a fox and a bear. A friendly bear, almost fatherly. Had she enough to read? Look, here were three books, lately published or reissued, one on the poems of Runeberg. She liked poetry? But no, no, no, he was stupid; it was in Swedish, it was not likely that she could read Swedish. Thomas Mann? That was in German, but perhaps she . . . No? A pity. The other book, unfortunately, would not interest her. It was written — he gave a brief awkward, apologetic bow — by himself. In Danish. He was a Dane, perhaps she had guessed? His name was Christian Thorwaldsen.

He paused to fumble in his pockets for a card. He found a crumpled letter, two crushed cigarettes, a half-torn check, some rubber bands, three ball-point pens, a pair of sunglasses with one pane missing, and several bank notes of

48

varying currencies. When these had been assembled on his tray, had fallen off and been retrieved by a steward, a stewardess, an old lady on her way to the lavatory and the passenger on the other side of the aisle, he concluded, regretfully, that he had left his cards behind in his house at Stockholm, where he was living at present in order to give a series of lectures.

"Or perhaps I left them in Paris, when I changed my airplane. Generally," he explained to Kerry, "my daughter is with me to look after me. She is very clever, very calm, very remem . . . she does not forget anything. But this time, I went by myself, and I think many things have been left behind."

Kerry, half-listening, saw with apprehension that coffee was being served; was this to be poured over her? But apart from dropping his spoon, the Professor, as she now knew him to be, managed without mishap. On her other side, the priest drank three cups, ate several biscuits and finished the packet of sweets. Prayer, but obviously no fasting, she thought grimly. And travelling in comfort, by air, probably to some place of pilgrimage, while the penitents did the journey on the ground, on their knees, for all he cared.

The Professor, his cup held firmly between his palms, studied her with a frank, serious, owlish stare. Then he asked if he might know her name.

"Catherine Cromer. I'm usually called Kerry."

"Kerry. Kerry Cromer. That is charming. As I told you, Miss Cromer, I am a professor of languages. I do not teach them; I study them. I write books about them. My books are published in Copenhagen and in Stockholm, but most of all in Paris, so I have to go there often, on business."

"Which languages?" Kerry asked, and immediately regretted asking. But it was too late. The Professor was already telling her.

"I am an authority on African dialects. I began with the four main divisions: Sudanic, Bantu, Semitic and Hamitic. Then I went on to deal with Temne or semi-Bantu. I have written on Ibo and Wolof, Hausa, also. I am just completing a work on the geographical groupings. Part One deals with Kru, Kwa, Mandingo and Niger-Chad. Then — please, Miss Cromer, say at once if what I am saying is not of interest to you. The second volume," he proceeded without pause, "will deal with the Atlantic coast tribes. In Part Three I shall deal with the semi-Bantu. Part Four will —"

At this point, there was a movement on Kerry's other side. Her first thought was that the priest, goaded to madness by this discourse, was about to clamber over them and lock himself in the lavatory. Instead, to her astonishment, he made a brief gesture of apology, leaned across her and, his eyes eager, his face flushed with excitement, addressed the Professor in French. The sentences were too rapid for her to follow, but their import was clear: the priest, too, dealt with Kru, Kwa, Mandingo and Niger-Chad.

Weak with relief, she gathered her things together, and after a shuffling exchange found herself seated by the window, free to press her nose against the pane and study the cloud effects and wait for the first sign of Nantes. The plane landed, taxied, stopped. The soft drone from the Professor went on. Even the business of disembarking did not interrupt the flow. The priest, all the while listening intently, saw to it that his companion's hat, books and newspapers were gathered up, thus preventing any interruption of the feast. Only at the customs counter was there a check, when the Professor, explaining a tricky point to the priest, pointed absently at the wrong suitcase and was soon afterward roused by the sight of ladies' underwear and the owner's loud protests. His farewell to Kerry was warm, but abstracted. Her last view of him, from the window of the taxi that bore her away to the station, was of his head bent close to the priest's, his hands behind his back, his lips moving.

Nantes did not impress her favourably, being, as far as she could see, entirely given up to industry. Nor did her spirits rise when a porter led her to the train in which she was to travel. No international giant this, conveying tourists in luxury coaches. It was short, crowded and had only two carriages that were labelled — misleadingly, she thought — first class. She chose the one that had three young children seated in it. The porter placed her suitcase on the rack and she paid him and then sat down to return the long, inquisitive stare directed at her by the three seated opposite. This might be fun, she thought. She liked children, and these looked intelligent and might be induced to talk at dictation speed. She was pleased to see, from their dawning smiles, that they approved of her; but she was not, after all, to travel with them. There was a shrill outcry from the platform. The children rushed to the window and there appeared a panting, agitated young couple easily identifiable as Papa and Mama. As easily, Kerry could understand what had occurred. This, cried Mama angrily, was what came of letting Grandmère come on ahead and secure a carriage for them. It was not this train — no, no, no! Out, out, before they were carried away who knew where? Out! Yes, yes, the baggage too, of course; did one leave baggage behind? Why, demanded Papa, had they taken so many things out of their cases even before the journey had begun? Where were Marie's books? Where was her other shoe? Where was Felipe's hat? Never mind, never mind; it would have to be abandoned; they must get out quickly. Come, come. Patrice, mind the step. Thank God there had been no delay in finding them! They had met Grandmère going away and she had told them she had put the children safely on the train. But they were not in the right train, and who knows what would have happened if — Ah, hurry!

They departed, leaving Kerry in a blank silence like that produced by switching off a too-loud commercial. Under the seat she spied a dusty, once-white sailor hat, and stooped and picked it up and pursued the rapidly retreating family. Having restored the hat, she was turning back to the carriage when she saw, some distance away, two familiar figures. They were coming in this direction, and her heart sank. Was she condemned to Kru and Kwa all over again?

She re-entered her carriage and closed the door. It was too much to expect that they would pass this, the only hope of empty seats. Perhaps it was the priest who was travelling, in which case there would be no lecture. If the Professor got in, she would get out her aspirins, sprinkle eau de Cologne on her handkerchief and act like a woman dying of migraine.

They appeared, stopped, looked in. The Professor exclaimed with pleasure. Here was Miss Cromer! How pleasant to be her travelling companion on this little journey. On the priest's face Kerry read relief at having found someone into whose care he could deliver the Professor for the final stage of the trip.

"His ticket is in order, mademoiselle," he assured her. "And he has a letter with the name and address of the person he is to visit. But he is not accustomed to arranging things for himself, and so . . ."

He had spoken in French, but very slowly and clearly, so that she might understand what he was saying. She nodded. A loud horn signalled the train's departure; it began to move, and she told herself that there was not much harm the old man could come to — unless he fell out of the window, which seemed likely as he leaned out perilously to see the last of the priest.

"A good man," he said at last, closing the window and sitting down. "A clever man, and also good. Do you know that he is going again to the Congo? He came back to Belgium for his health. Now it is restored, and he is going back. When he heard me speaking of my work, he was —" He paused, his eyes on the small package Kerry was replacing in her bag. "Aspirins?"

"Yes. I thought I was going to get a —"

"You have a headache? And here I am talking —"

"It's better. I just —"

"You must have suffered by this noise I have been making! Always, I run on, forgetting myself. May I advise that you lean back and close your eyes? I will pull down this sunshade and you will not be troubled by the glare."

"Thank you, but I'm all right. All I —"

"I shall say nothing to disturb you. I shall read my books, I shall make notes on some things the priest told me. You must remain quiet. May I ask if you are going far on this train?"

"I'm going as far as Gaston-le-Grand."

She did not need to be told that he, too, was going as far as Gaston-le-Grand; the joy on his countenance was enough.

"I, too! How fortunate that is for me, that we

shall be going together! Who would have imagined, who could have guessed that two people would get on to an airplane in Paris, would sit next to one another and would prove, at last, to be going to this place that I have never before heard of and that the priest told me is not at all important? But perhaps you already knew about it?"

"No. I've never been there."

"You are going to visit friends?"

"No. This is a business trip."

"Business! So young, and if I may be permitted to say this, so very, very pretty — to go on business! Today, women are so capable, so independent, just like my daughter, who has been my guardian, I will not say my keeper, for nearly twenty years. She travels with me everywhere, she packs my bag, she buys my tickets, she sees which train, which airplane — everything. But this time, I have come without her because . . . well, because this is a very special journey for me, and I wished to come alone. I wished — But you have a headache, and I promised that I would make no disturbance. I advise that you should close your eyes and be quiet. It is a pity that we did not drive through Nantes together. It is very interesting. Once I stayed there for many months. Did you know that it was in Nantes that Henry IV signed the edict giving religious freedom to the Huguenots?"

"Yes. At school —"

"Ah! At school, it all seems dull, no? And then

one is actually in the place which was only a dull fact in a history book, and then it begins to be real. Nantes, you know, was once the capital of the Gallic tribes of the Namnetes."

Here it came, she thought. Namnetes, Kru, Kwa.

"It was only in 1491 that Nantes came under French rule. I wish we could have arranged that I had time to show you the town. But this would have been impossible, since we had to catch this train. Will you stay long in Gaston-le-Grand?"

"No."

"I have only three days to spare, after that I must go back. Is your headache a little better?"

She nodded. It was impossible to be angry. Even the irritation he had roused in her was dying away. She did not envy his daughter, but there was something about his simplicity and helplessness that was appealing. Behind his spectacles, his eyes looked out at her, blue and mild and anxious. His clothes were beginning to look travel-worn, but somebody — the daughter, no doubt — saw to it that his linen was spotless, his hands well cared for, his shoes polished. When he stood up to take his suitcase down from the rack and opened it and displayed its meticulously folded garments, she felt a wave of liking for the unknown woman who looked after him so well.

"I am getting out something to show you," he said, and to her dismay began to rummage among the contents like a dog scratching up sand. "It is a map I bought in Paris, which shows the district through which we are now travelling. I like" — he turned and bent his head and gave her one of his characteristic, solemn stares from over his glasses — "I like to know where I am going, don't you? All I knew about this Gaston-le-Grand, before I spoke of it to the priest, was that it was beside the sea. But for some reason" — he resumed his search with increased energy — "for some reason, it does not seem to be here. Perhaps I put it into my pockets. I do not think so, but then often, my daughter says, I do not think properly what I am doing."

He sat down and began to search his pockets. She saw him frown and heard a low murmur of dismay. His expression became agitated, and then panic-stricken. Abandoning the search through his pockets, he returned to the suitcase, this time completely emptying it, bundling garments onto the seat, disregarding objects that slid to the floor.

Kerry watched him uneasily, unable to bear the sight of the neat, expensive garments being mangled. But it was not her business. It would be his daughter's job to clean up the dusty handkerchiefs and unsnarl the ties and restore the beautiful shirts to their original whiteness.

Then he turned to her, and she was shocked by the pallor of his face.

"It is lost!"

She stared up at him.

"The map?"

Bewilderment drove the panic for a moment

57

from his countenance.

"Map? I do not understand," he faltered. "Did you say a map?"

"You were looking for a map, weren't you?"

"Oh — that. Yes, at first. At first I think that I was doing that, looking for a map. I do not remember which map. But then I thought of the letter. It is not in my pockets. It is not in my luggage. It is nowhere! It is lost!"

"A letter?"

He sat down heavily. His hair was wildly disarranged, and he drew a shaky hand over it to smooth it. He took a handkerchief absently from the pile Kerry was picking up from the floor, and wiped the beads of perspiration from his forehead.

"It is lost!" he moaned. "It is lost! And without it, how shall I know, where shall I go? It was written there, but I cannot remember what it was. What shall I do?" He was staring at her with eyes that looked blind. "I will tell you now, I will confess that this is my fault for having for the first time deceived my daughter. I came without her, and I did not tell her where I was going. I said only, in a little note which I put on to her worktable, that I was going on a little journey and she must not worry about me. I wished for certain reasons to come alone. And you see what has happened! I am here, and I have forgotten why! No, not forgotten why. Only the name and the address. What shall I do?"

Her determination to avoid involvement faded

and died. She heard herself speaking in a voice of calm reassurance.

"If you'll tell me exactly what it is you're looking for, I'll help you to go through your things properly. It's no use scrambling through them as you've been doing."

He gave a vague glance at the disorder he had created. Then he faced her, forlorn, helpless, awaiting orders.

"Please tell me," she went on firmly, "exactly what it is you've lost."

"My — my wallet."

"Was all your money in it?"

"Money?" He peered at her in bewilderment. "Oh, money. Oh, no, no, no; money is all right. I have those things — those as they are called Traveller's Cheques. No, it is not because of money that I am worried."

"Then — ?"

"I . . ." He swallowed. "It is a letter. One page only. I received this letter, and I kept it because it had on it a name and address. I do not remember the name and I do not remember the address. When I left home, I had it. In my wallet."

"And since leaving home, where have you been?"

"In the airplane."

"Before that, where?"

"In Paris, for two hours only. I went to the bank and . . ." He held a hand to his head. "Perhaps there, in Paris, in the bank . . . But how can I get it, if it is there?"

"We could telephone to the bank and ask if they had found your wallet."

We? Had she said we? Why not? she thought resignedly. It would continue to be We until the wallet was found and until she could deliver him to the lost address.

"But there is no time!" he pointed out. "If they have it, how shall they send it so soon?"

"First, we'll make a thorough search," she said. "Please will you look carefully — no, not like that — *slowly* through your pockets."

There was certainly no wallet there. She put him aside and began to repack the suitcase, replacing each article, each garment carefully after she had ascertained that no wallet had concealed itself in a fold or in a pocket. The case grew full; the last garment was neatly replaced. The train stopped at one, two, three stations. People glanced in, but nobody entered. How many more stations before they reached Gaston-le-Grand? Two, she thought.

She closed the suitcase, locked it, gave the key to the Professor and sat down.

"No wallet," she confirmed. "So no address. As soon as we get to Gaston-le-Grand, we'll find a place for you to stay. Then you must telephone to the bank and find out if they've found the wallet. It's too late to telephone to them today, but you can do it tomorrow morning. If they have it, would you ask them to open it and see if the letter's inside? If it is, they can read you the name and address."

He looked at her like a thirst-racked fugitive who had at last come upon a mirage that was wet to the touch. Closer to home, it was how her Aunt Sylvia looked at the piano when she crossed her left hand gracefully over the right and found that she had landed on the right note. Or how George looked when Dale came into a room.

"How can I thank you, Miss Cromer?"

"There's nothing to thank me for. I wish I'd been staying longer."

"I, too, wish that. But you have made me see what I have to do, and I am grateful. I am sorry that I was so foolish as to lose my head, but I was frightened. I have come a long way to see a very old friend, a friend very dear to me, and to lose the letter . . ."

So dear and so old a friend, Kerry reflected, that he couldn't even remember his name. She saw the train slowing down, and began to gather her things. Together they sat waiting for the moment of arrival.

"Please try to believe me," the Professor begged, his manner, to her relief, more self-possessed. "I am not so stupid as I seem. For my work, my brain is adequate. But for other things, things which are always changing, like how is this telephone number, who is the butcher, the baker, how much gas is in the car, is more money needed from the bank, who is having a reception on this or that day — for these things I have no head, and they are left to my daughter. She is like you — calm, never fussing, clever to remember everything, always cheerful. She makes appointments for me, she sees that I keep them. She travels with me. Only this time, I came alone — foolishly. And without you to reassure me, to help me, where would I be?"

She did not reply. She had risen and was leaning out of the window, reading the name of the station at which the train was about to stop.

"Gaston-le-Grand," she announced. "We're here."

A porter came to help them, and she was glad to be able to leave directions to the Professor. She hesitated over leaving her suitcase in the station cloakroom, and decided to take it with her; what she could see of Gaston-le-Grand looked unprepossessing, so if she could hand over Lord Hazing's message without being held up, there might be time to catch a late train back to Nantes, where she would have a wider choice of hotels.

They walked out in warm sunshine to a line of decrepit taxis, when the Professor said that he wished to be taken to a good hotel, the driver grinned. The Splendide, he said, was the only hotel; they could take it or leave it.

They got into the taxi and Kerry, staring out at the streets along which they were driving, had a feeling of being cheated. This was a French town, a smallish French town, but unmistakably a French town, with the *epiceries* and the *charcuteries* and the *boulangeries* that had appeared in the illustrations in her early French textbooks but where was the colour? The shops should have been scarlet-and-white. The shopkeepers should have been short and rotund and rosy-cheeked. Where were the children bowling bright red hoops, where the nursemaids with flying cap ribbons? And, since this was a seaside town, though nobody would have guessed it, where was the gay little harbour with its tree-shaded waterfront? Where were the busy little cafés filled with bearded young students? Where was the bandstand? Where were the little girls with big straw hats and high laced boots? Did it exist, that bright and laughing land? All she had seen was an airport, and an industrial district and this seedy little town.

The taxi drew up on one side of a crowded but unimposing avenue. This, the driver informed them, was the main street, the town center; there was the Hotel Splendide.

They got out and looked at it. Two of the letters of its name were missing, so that it had become the Hotel Sp . end . de. It occupied a meager frontage between a chemist's shop and a barber's. No, the taxi driver reiterated in response to their question, there was no other hotel. Some *pensions;* he could take them to look at them — but there was not another hotel. There had been one, but it had burned down.

Inside the hotel, things looked better. It was small, but it shone with cleanliness, and through the lace curtains of the dining room opening off the hall, they could see tables covered with snow-white cloths and a sideboard laden with baskets of fruit. It might call itself a splendid hotel, but it was in fact a pleasant little family one.

"This is good." The Professor looked around with a visible lightening of spirit. "You shall leave me here and I shall give you no more trouble. To-morrow I shall telephone to the bank and I shall ask them what you advised, and then perhaps they will give me the name and the address. But even if the wallet is lost, I think that I shall not be lost, because very often in the past, I have forgotten something because of the confusion of travel, and in the morning, after a good rest, I have remembered everything. Here in this clean hotel I shall be quiet, I shall rest and eat and sleep, and by tomorrow I am sure that I shall have remembered the name and address."

He accompanied her to the waiting taxi and took her hands in his.

"I cannot thank you, Miss Cromer, but if you would be kind enough to tell me where you live, my daughter would like to write to you."

She wrote the address of her London flat, tore the page out of her diary and gave it to him. As the taxi moved away, she had an impulse to go back and assure him that she would get in touch with him on her way back to the station. Then she reflected that he was perfectly capable of telephoning to Paris; if he did not obtain the lost address and did not manage to recall it, all he had to do was make his way back to Nantes and get on a plane and fly home.

She brought her mind back to her own affairs. Gaston-le-Grand, she saw, was improving. There was still no sign of the sea, but the taxi was climbing around the shoulder of a low hill, and she had a glimpse of blue. There was a momentary darkness as they drove through a thick pinewood, and then they were in sunlight once more, and she was gazing out at a scene so beautiful that she heard herself gasp.

Every evidence of the busy, second-rate town had vanished. The road they were on was a private one, giving access only to four large, solidly built houses standing on the summit of the hill and protected by the pinewood, which swept down almost to sea level. Before each house, a gap had been cut through the trees to give an unimpeded view; also in front of each house was a zigzag path leading down to the road below, which curved around a small, golden beach and ended at a little harbour crowded with gaily painted dinghies, some fishing boats and three white motor yachts. Beyond the harbour ran a line of rocks, which cut off a very much larger, very much more popular beach, which lay on the other side. Along it, Kerry could see all the amenities missing from the beach at the foot of the hill: cafés, shops, shelters, restaurants.

As they drove slowly past the houses, she read the names painted on the low, white boards in front of each one. Maison Gabrielle. Villa Azul.

These two were closed and shuttered, but their gardens were neat and well tended. Miramar. Here there were signs of life — curtains fluttering, a maid pulling up blinds.

And then the fourth house. Maison du Bois. Well named, she thought. A little smaller than the others, but like them, stone-built and capable of resisting the winter winds that must blow through the gaps in the pinewood. A neat front lawn. A white wicker gate.

She asked the driver to wait and got out. Despite the house's strength and solidity, she thought it had an attractively feminine look; there was a verandah with a curly white railing, and roses climbed the pillars beside the front door. It looked welcoming, smiling, homey. Not at all the setting, she reflected, for one of Lord Hazing's ex-mistresses, who in her experience settled themselves, or allowed him to settle them in comfortable London apartments within reach of the most fashionable boutiques.

She lifted the latch of the gate. At one of the windows, behind muslin curtains, she caught a glimpse of a stout form that she decided was Madame Daumier — though if she had been that shape fifteen years ago, there would certainly have been no romance. Lord Hazing did not care for overweights.

The book he had sent was in her hand. More than ever, it seemed a poor present compared with the expense of getting it here. But the message written inside it must have some significance known only to the writer and the recipient, and now she would deliver it.

She paused at the neat front door and pulled the hanging bell rope. There was a deep clang followed by heavy footsteps. Kerry summoned her carefully prepared phrases.

The door opened. Stout indeed was the form, but it was clad in a well-fitting black dress with a narrow lace collar and a white apron with a pleated bib. A white cap rested on a little gray topknot.

The phrases had not been sufficiently well re-hearsed.

"Madame Daumier?" was all that came out.

It was enough. The door opened wide; Kerry was ushered into a large, softly carpeted hall.

"Mademoiselle's name?"

Kerry had written it on a small blank card. *Miss C. Cromer.* The maid took it, put it onto a small silver salver and placed a chair for the visitor. There was time to look around and note the beautiful console table, a tall narrow Norman cupboard, a massive old chest with a bowl of flowers standing on it. Then the maid was back, ushering her along a corridor. A soft knock, a soft voice speaking in reply. The maid stood aside for Kerry to enter and withdrew, closing the door behind her.

Kerry took two paces. Against the window was a rather small, slim form and a face shadowed by the curtains that were half-drawn to keep out the rays of the setting sun.

"Madame Daumier? Do you by any chance speak —"

She stopped, and she could not have spoken again, in English or in French or in any language. For the figure had moved, and had come out of the shadow, had advanced and then, like herself, had halted abruptly. And Kerry was staring not at a stranger, not at an unknown Frenchwoman, but at her sister Dale. Dale in every last detail. Dale's eyes, nose, mouth. Dale's fair hair, Dale's white skin. Nothing, no, nothing whatsoever of Elvira. Simply Dale.

And when she spoke, Dale's voice, though it faltered.

"K—K—*Kerry?*"

That was all. Silence fell, and the two stood immobile, unable to do more than stare at one another. Madame Daumier's mouth was open, her eyes were blue and blank.

And at last Kerry understood that if there were to be any suggestion of moving, it would have to come from herself; Madame Daumier appeared paralyzed.

"I think," she said, and was surprised at the quietness, the calmness of her voice, "I think we had both better sit down."

Chapter Three

When, weeks later, Kerry attempted to recall for Dale's benefit all that she had felt on entering the drawing room of the Maison du Bois and recognizing her mother, nothing emerged but bare facts. Perhaps the impressions made by the encounter had by then been erased by the experiences that followed so closely upon them — but there was justification for Dale's protest at being told that the first clear thought that had emerged from the confusion in Kerry's mind on that historic occasion was that a taxi was waiting.

"Oh, Kerry! That can't be true!"

It was true enough. Madame Daumier, seated, had been as speechless as she had been when standing up. Her eyes, fixed on Kerry, were blank; her mouth remained open. And Kerry, gazing at her, realized that the likeness to Dale was fading, or merging into a smudged portrait of Dale. There was a softness in the mouth and in the line of chin that Dale had never had and never would have. There was the same undeniable beauty, but none of Dale's animation or Dale's intelligence. It was perhaps not fair to assume that Madame Daumier would always look as moronic as she was looking at this moment, but nothing about her suggested mental agility.

It was with relief that Kerry saw some colour return to the pale cheeks and some expression to the blank blue eyes.

"Oh Kerry" — a long, shuddering sigh stirred the lace ruffles on Madame Daumier's breast — "you should have warned me."

"Warned? But I had no idea —"

"It's such a terrible shock. I feel very shaky. You should have — well, you should have prepared me."

"I couldn't have prepared you, because until I walked in —"

"That's what I mean. To walk in without preparing me. If you'd only given me a little time."

"But I had no idea who you were — until I came in and saw you."

Madame Daumier drew her brows together; it could hardly be called a frown. Her voice took on a faintly plaintive note.

"But if you didn't know me, why did you come?"

"I was sent."

"There you are, you see. If you were sent, you must have known whom you were being sent to. Perhaps if you'd written something when Clothilde asked for your name, some word of warning, I wouldn't have got such a terrible shock when I saw you."

"How did you know who I was?"

"It was just like seeing your father." She shuddered. "Shocks are very upsetting. Just walking in like —"

"That reminds me," Kerry said. "I didn't walk. I came in a taxi and it's waiting outside. I think perhaps I'd better pay the man and send him away. Could someone bring my suitcase in?"

"Suitcase?"

"After seeing you, I was going on to the station, to go back to Nantes."

"Nantes?"

The echo would have been irritating if Madame Daumier had not looked like a bewildered child attempting to follow a difficult conversation. Kerry had always considered forty-five an age not far off the foot-in-grave period, but who could call this woman old? Soft, wavy hair simply arranged, small blue ear-studs, a minimum of makeup, clothes that fitted rather than flowed. And not one unnecessary movement or gesture, except that now and then a hand came up in a slow, graceful wave to emphasize a word, returning to nestle inside its fellow in her lap. It all added up to form a charming picture. But if they were to proceed beyond these preliminaries, Kerry realized that she would have to provide the initiative.

"I think I'd better send the taxi away," she said.

"Yes. Will you press that bell?"

It was nearer to Madame Daumier than it was to Kerry, who had to walk across in order to reach it. She pressed it, and Clothilde appeared. In French not much better than Kerry's, Madame Daumier asked her to pay the driver and bring in the suitcase. And after that, she added,

Clothilde could bring coffee and brandy.

"I need something to drink," she told Kerry when the door had closed behind the maid. "I can't remember when I've had such a dreadful shock."

"I'm sorry. But I was sent with a message from Lord Hazing."

This forthright statement, she saw at once, was a mistake. It sent Madame Daumier back to her state of paralysis. It would have been better to go outside and write it down and send it by Clothilde. Fifteen years was fifteen years, and to appear from the past without a word of warning was just the sort of inconsiderate behaviour to be expected of Lord Hazing. Fifteen years. Thank God, that ruled him out as a possible father. It was bad enough to discover that her mother was his ex-mistress.

How could he have fallen in love with this childish, wide-eyed, woolly-witted woman? Beauty — yes, there was that, but at the least failure to follow his orders or his reasoning, he went into a state bordering on frenzy. Kerry had known nothing of his first wife, but the second had been as shrewd as she was soignée. How could he have endured listening to this plaintive echo?

Madame Daumier was speaking in a faint voice.

"*That,*" she said, "was something you should have told me as soon as you came in."

"Perhaps when I saw you I stopped thinking

very clearly. I should have explained that I work for Lord Hazing. I've been working for him for about a year. He met with an accident — not a serious one, just his ankle, so —"

"You . . . work for him?"

"I'm his secretary. He couldn't come himself, so he sent me with a —"

"Come *himself*? Come *himself*? You mean he was coming *here*?"

There was such pure horror in the tone that Kerry was glad to see the door open and the coffee — and especially the brandy — appear on a large silver tray that Clothilde placed on the table. As Madame Daumier made no move toward it, Kerry poured out two cups, laced them generously with brandy and carried one to her mother.

"Thank you." Madame Daumier took it and gazed up at Kerry. "Did you say that he was coming here?"

"He was going to, but he couldn't with an injured ankle."

Madame Daumier drew a long breath of relief.

"To think of coming, without warning, after fifteen years. I don't think he would have done that."

"Then he must have changed since you knew him. It's just the kind of thing he would do. All he told me was that I was to come here in his place, and bring you a book."

"A *book*?"

Kerry picked the book up and took it to her. Madame Daumier opened it and read the message, but her look of bewilderment proved that it meant nothing to her.

"Is that all he said? Just that you were to bring me a book?"

"That was all."

A sense of fantasy gripped Kerry, making her wonder if the scene was really being enacted. A mother and daughter united after twenty years. Instant recognition. And then not one word of inquiry from the mother, not one word of the past, of her other child. Not a word about Thea or Sylvia or Dulcie or Elvira, who had brought up her children.

The thought of her aunts seemed to provide the final touch of fantasy. Four down-to-earth, capable, sturdy, independent daughters — and then Madeleine, with more beauty than all the others put together, but with no more than half an ounce of brain. She couldn't be expected to cope with a daughter, an ex-lover and a book with an incomprehensible message, not all together. Not all at once. She was not perhaps unfeeling, perhaps not totally devoid of maternal instinct; she was merely incapable of dealing with more than one idea at a time. So it was no use releasing the flood of questions that were welling up. It was no use attempting to prise open the past, to trace the long road that had begun at a large, shabby English house and ended, if this was the end, in a large, luxurious French one. There was no point in putting any questions at all, for something in her mother's manner was beginning to reveal to Kerry that behind the blank, bewildered look was a caution, a caginess that would come very near secrecy. If the past were unveiled, it would be unveiled in discreet sections.

Madame Daumier put down her empty cup.

"How," she asked, "did you know me as soon as you came into the room?"

"Because you're the image of Dale."

"I suppose you and she often wondered about — well, about your father?"

"Now and then."

There was a pause.

"I don't think," Madame Daumier said at last, "that I can tell you anything about him until I've written to ask, well, whether he'd mind."

Kerry said nothing. What, she wondered, could you reply to a remark like that? The only one that occurred to her was that if and when he had decided to acknowledge his children, his children should be approached in order to find out whether they wished to acknowledge him

"Did your aunts — did they talk about me?" Madame Daumier inquired.

"Yes. That's how I knew that Dale looked so much like you."

"Does Dale work, too?"

"She's married. She's going to have a baby in September."

Another mistake, she saw at once. Never announce the imminence of grandmotherhood without first writing a note and sending it in.

Unasked, she rose and poured out more coffee for her mother.

"Thank you." Madame Daumier spoke faintly. "That was rather a shock. I don't think I feel like a grandmother."

In anybody else, Kerry thought, this would sound like the vapours, but her mother's manner was disarming because it held not the least trace of affectation.

"You don't look like a grandmother," she said. "Didn't the message that Lord Hazing wrote in the book mean anything to you?"

"No. Are you quite, quite sure that's all he said?"

"Quite, quite sure. He never does say anything, in the sense you mean. He merely issues orders. I don't know what he was like fifteen years ago, but today, he's a big bully."

"Bully?"

"Yes. Was he better tempered when he was younger?"

"I — well, he liked his own way. All the same, I wouldn't have called him —"

"— a bully? Well, he is. Why has he suddenly decided to get in touch with you after all this time?"

Madame Daumier stared. She was a great starer, Kerry decided. Big, blue eyes on the questioner while she debated how or what to answer, if anything. But when the answer came at last, it surprised Kerry.

"I wrote him."

This time Kerry realized that it was she who was staring. Perhaps it ran in families.

"You wrote to him? There was nothing in the files."

"Files?"

"I'm his confidential secretary. I see most —"

"Files!"

"He likes to keep things straight. I have to —"

"Files? You mean," Madame Daumier breathed in horror, "you mean that you see his — well, his *personal* papers?"

"Some of them. Don't ask me what makes employers know they can rely absolutely on their confidential secretaries' discretion, but they do. Maybe that's why we come so expensive."

"Files!"

"Only while the affair's going on. When it's over, I'm told to destroy it. I saw nothing from you, so you must be special. I suppose he decided to answer your letter in person."

"I hope you never found anything about me in a file."

"No. If I had, the name Daumier wouldn't have meant anything. How long did you manage to stick — I mean, were you with — that's to say, did you know Lord Hazing for long?"

Madame Daumier considered.

"I left him fifteen years ago," she said at last. "But it wasn't a question of 'sticking' him, Kerry. We had three very happy years together in Paris. Are you absolutely sure that he didn't send a letter or anything?"

77

"No letter. If the message he wrote doesn't mean anything, there must be something in the book itself that'll clear it up."

"Perhaps. Will you ring the bell, please?"

Kerry rang, and the tray was removed.

"Why did you call yourself Cromer?" Madame Daumier asked, when the door had closed.

"It was Elvira's name. You knew she married?"

"She told me she was going to, but I don't remember hearing his name." She paused. "Were you and Dale happy?"

There were some questions Kerry felt she might have put in response to that one: Did you care? Did you ever wonder if we were? Would you have done anything about it if we hadn't been? Instead, she said: "Yes. We were very happy."

"Did you wonder why I gave you up to your aunts?"

"Not once we knew a few facts-of-life. Dragging us around couldn't have been easy. You told Elvira enough to make her realize that you were never in one place for long."

"You must have blamed me for deserting you."

"We didn't."

Madame Daumier stared at her for a time.

"I don't know whether you mean that or not," she said finally. "I don't think you always say everything you're thinking."

This flash of perception startled Kerry.

"You may be right," she admitted. "It's probably a kind of protective shell that I've grown

78

since I went out to work. It's been a great help in deflecting the barbs my employers directed at me. I earn fabulous salaries because I work for men like Lord Hazing. You need a shell."

"Did you answer an advertisement?"

"Before going to work for him? No. I'd done some work for one of his competitors, and he asked the agency to let him know if I was ever available. I didn't like him, but the salary he offered was so high that I decided to take on the job."

"Do you live at Orchard House?"

"No. I may look like my father, but there must be something of you in me, because — like you — I wanted to get away. That's one thing I always understood about you, the need to get away."

"Do you go back often?"

"Yes. But if you're picturing the place as it was —"

"No. I passed close to it once, and I saw that there wasn't any open country left. But when I was there, it was like living in a sort of desert, miles and miles and miles from anything or anybody. I can't explain properly."

"You don't have to."

"It was different for the others. They liked it. They never wanted to go outside the garden walls. I don't suppose they ever have?"

"No."

"It was no use saying anything, because they wouldn't have understood. Not even my father would have understood. You never knew him. He was a —"

"I know. The aunts kept telling us. He was a dear, kind, scholarly — and so on."

"I loved him very much. He gave me lessons to do, but I didn't understand them and he couldn't explain very well because he was getting old. I used to make dolls' houses out of shells when I was supposed to be doing sums. It was lonely, because the others all seemed to be grown-up; old, really. I used to like to stay with my father in his study. He had a beautiful white head, and there were hundreds and hundreds of books on the shelves all around the room, and there was a big window and you could look out and see the fruit trees, and the birds. I couldn't have gone away while he was alive, so I waited until he died."

There was a pause. Madame Daumier was sitting as motionless as ever, but her gaze was on the expanse of sea beyond the little beach.

"And then?" Kerry asked quietly.

"Then? Then I went away. I didn't say anything to the others. I don't think they would have tried to stop me, but I wanted to get right away. And I knew that I'd never go back."

"Did you just walk out, with no plans?"

"Plans?"

"Did you know what you were going to do?"

"Oh, plans. No. I went to London because it seemed the place where there were most people. When I got there, I asked the taxi driver to take me to an agency."

"Agency?" Yes, it did run in families.

"An employment agency. I thought they'd tell me what jobs they had, and then I'd see if I could do any of them. But there didn't seem to be anything, except for trained people, and I wasn't trained. The only thing they could think of was parlour maids, who were very scarce, so I said I'd try that, and they sent me to a house to be interviewed. I got there and I was standing checking the name when the door opened and a man came out. He shut the door behind him and I shut the gate behind me, and we stood looking at one another."

"Dale's father?"

"And yours."

"Why didn't you marry him?"

Madame Daumier hesitated, and Kerry realized that she was trying to decide how much she would say in answer to the question. When she spoke again, her tone had changed; it was absent, almost dreamy; she was recalling, revealing the past.

"Because he had a wife. She lived in their house in the country, and it was there that I was going to try to be a parlour maid, only I never got there. He happened to be staying in town and . . . well, that's how it was. He took a flat in Kensington and Dale was born there. She was named after your father's mother. You were born in Ireland, which is why your father always called you Kerry."

"Was it his idea to hand us over to the aunts?"

"No. It was mine. I did it because I realized I

was never going to have a settled home. Your father had to move about all the time. I didn't know it then, but every man I fell in love with was going to be a man who had to move about all the time. And all I wanted was a settled home. I wanted a house where I could live as we never lived at Orchard House — a house where the meals were on time, where the furniture was polished, where things were always in their right places, where the rugs didn't have holes and the curtains weren't patched. All I wanted was a man who'd come home from an office every evening and go to work next day and every day. And it always looked, at first, as though I'd got one — and then he'd be sent to, or he had business in, some place thousands of miles away, and we'd be on the move again. When I met your father, he was settled — but not for long. Until you were nearly two, I followed him about — to America, to Venezuela, to Chile. Then I realized it wasn't a life for babies, and the only place I could think of that was permanent was Orchard House. I knew your aunts would love you and look after you, and leave you free to grow up in your own way, as they'd left me. So I decided to ask them to keep you. But your father, who was in Chile, didn't agree and I don't know what I would have done about it if I hadn't heard that he was living with another woman. I wrote and asked Elvira to meet me and I handed you both over, and I never regretted it because until I came to this house I never had a settled home of any kind."

She stopped, and seemed to fall into a reverie, and Kerry let her eyes roam around the drawing room of the settled home in which the wanderer had come to rest. It looked very comfortable. And not a bad finish — she felt shame at the thought, but could not thrust it away — not a bad finish for one who had set out to be a parlour maid. And as strange as this end was this beginning to a mother-daughter relationship. She had wondered, sometimes to herself, sometimes in talk with Dale, how they would behave if they ever came across one parent, or both. Nothing they had envisaged came near to this meeting, in which two strangers, one young and the other middle-aged, conducted a calm conversation during which not one word of warmth or affection had been uttered on either side. Try as she would, Kerry could not bring herself to realize that this woman was her mother, bound to her by the closest of all ties. She felt nothing but a vague regret, and another emotion that might — she could not imagine why — be pity, or protectiveness. There seemed not the slightest need for either.

There was another question to be asked.

"Monsieur Daumier?" she ventured.

It drew another blank stare.

"Who?"

"Monsieur Daumier. Is he . . ."

"No. There was never any Monsieur Daumier," said Madame Daumier.

"Then — ?"

"We thought it would be more discreet if I came here as the widow of a Frenchman. It was really Albert's idea."

Yes, this was fantasy, Kerry decided. Or a play. Enter Al, bare.

"Albert?"

"Albert Leclair. You must know the name. He was famous. World-famous."

Kerry went through her file of world-famous personalities and rejected Leclair's French Pastry Mix and Leclair's Gallic Night Cream, to come upon a dim memory of a school lecture on orchestras.

"Leclair the conductor?"

Her mother nodded, pleased.

"Yes. I knew you must have heard of him. Albert Leclair. He brought me here."

"Does he own this house?"

"No. Madame Courbet owned it, but she died two months ago. That's why I —"

She stopped, but Kerry waited with such patent expectancy that after some moments, she completed the sentence.

"That's why I wrote to Lord Hazing."

"Did Lord Hazing know Madame Courbet?"

"Oh goodness, no. She lived here, next door to this house. She and her husband. He went to Paris last week, but he'll be back tomorrow. That's why I hoped —"

"Yes?"

"That's why I hoped Lord Hazing would have —"

"Would have — ?"

"I hoped he would have answered my letter, that's all."

"And you're certain that book isn't some kind of reply?"

"How could it be?" Madame Daumier's hand rose and seemed to draw a question mark in the air. "Why should he send a book when what I'd asked for was —"

"Was — ?"

"Money."

The word was brought out with the greatest reluctance. Kerry sat considering the pieces of the puzzle, but could make nothing of them. She was using the wrong technique, she decided. She would try the correction-of-mistakes method.

"You wrote and told Lord Hazing that Madame Courbet had died, but that her husband would be back tomorrow and —"

"Oh, no. If Madame Courbet hadn't died, I wouldn't have needed the money. Or really, if she hadn't died, Edouard wouldn't have needed the money. It was all hers, you see; he had hardly anything when they married. I could only pay him a deposit, but I told him that when he came back from Paris, I'd give him the rest of the money."

"Money for what, exactly?"

"To buy this house."

"It isn't yours?"

"No. I told you. Albert brought me here. It always belonged to Madame Courbet, but she'd never agree to selling. She used to let it. Albert had rented it for years, summer after summer. He always came in June with his wife and his son, and they stayed until the end of September, though sometimes he had to go away for concerts. He and I met in Paris, and we fell in love and his wife took it very badly and went to Switzerland, taking the son with her, and I came down here with Albert. It worked out very well, because he was giving up conducting and was planning to start a school for conductors, in Paris. That's what he's doing now. But while he was here with me, he bought a farmhouse just outside the town, and made it into a free hostel where young musicians could come and compose, or practice, or rest. Then later he included painters, because his son took up painting and not music, as Albert had hoped. So we were very happy here, and when Albert went back to his wife, he tried to buy the house for me because I liked it so much and wanted to stay in it — but Madame Courbet said she'd never sell it. And she didn't. But she left it to Edouard. Not her money, because that had to go to the children of her first husband. Then Edouard came and told me he wanted to sell it, and I was to have the first offer. Now do you see?"

"Yes, I think so. And you paid a deposit, and wrote to Lord Hazing to ask for the remainder?"

"And got a book. That's why I think he must have said something else to you. Or perhaps not. Perhaps he was still angry, and had never for-

86

given me for leaving him. But why send a book?"

"Is the furniture yours?"

"Yes. I wish you could have seen this place when I first came. Madame Courbet had furnished it for holiday lets, and it was full of bamboo chairs and dreadful beds and the walls upstairs were covered with peculiar pictures done by Albert's son. But I couldn't change anything because I thought I might have to move if Albert's wife ever wanted to come back. But she said she would never enter the house again, and when Albert went back to her, I sent to Paris for the furniture that Lord Hazing had put into store when I left him. It was hard to get Madame Courbet to agree to clear out all her awful things, but in the end she did, and she gave me permission to redecorate. And now I want to buy it and live in it always. So that's why I wrote to Lord Hazing. I told you that all I ever wanted was a settled home. This home. I would never have left your father if he had agreed to let me stay in one place while he moved around, but he wouldn't hear of it. *I* had to be, he said, wherever *he* was. And in the end, I couldn't bear it. And now I don't know what Edouard will say when he comes back tomorrow and —"

She stopped. Tomorrow was the future, and Kerry was here and would presumably be part of it.

"You won't have to go away at once, will you?" she asked.

"I'm on my way to Tours."

"On another errand for Lord Hazing?"

"No. Just a date."

"A man?"

"Yes. As a matter of fact, the man who wrote that book. Nigel Frame."

"Is it serious?"

"That sounded exactly like Dale. I don't know whether it's serious or not."

"Aren't you in love with him?"

Kerry smiled.

"I was hoping to find out."

"You're not sure?"

"I'm almost sure I'm not."

"Then Kerry, will you stay here for a little while? Even just for a few days. We haven't really talked about anything. I haven't asked about Dale, or about her husband, or about your aunts. You're here, your luggage is here. Please stay! Unless — well, unless you'd rather go away. Would you?"

"No. I'd rather stay," Kerry said.

Chapter Four

Some time during the night, Kerry stirred and remembered, dimly, two figures from a past in which only the members of her family seemed real. Nigel, and Professor Thorwaldsen. They were both waiting for something; for what, she would no doubt recall in the morning. Too much had happened too fast. Her brain was confused.

Last night there had been dinner, and coffee on the balcony that overlooked the beach and the harbour. She and her mother had talked; that is, she had talked and her mother had listened, leaning back in her chair, motionless, attentive, only occasionally joining in to clear up or to create confusion. They had parted at midnight, no longer strangers but still far removed from intimacy. Theirs was not a mother-daughter relationship, and Kerry was sure that it never would be. She doubted whether even Dale, so much more than herself inclined to tolerance and charity, would award their mother prizes for wit or intelligence. What there had been to attract men of sense and achievement, perhaps no woman was competent to judge.

She wakened early and lay looking out at the sunlit sea, as last night she had lain gazing at the winking lights of the little harbour. The dinghies were fidgeting restlessly, the yachts dipping gracefully from time to time. Farther out, the fishing boats rose and fell on the gentle waves.

Clothilde brought her breakfast in bed, perhaps to keep her from descending too soon and putting a check on the cleaning activities audible when the bedroom door opened. That would be Marie, who was Clothilde's daughter. Clothilde's husband was butler, handyman and gardener. Between them they ran the house and relieved Madame Daumier of every responsibility save that of ordering the meals. Not an inexpensive establishment, Kerry mused, eating toast and *croissants* and honey and wondering why she was so much hungrier here than at home. No, not an economical setup. Rent, three servants, beautiful clothes, no sign of any books, but a great many glossy, high-priced magazines. There was no noticeable lack of money, but she could understand that though there might be capital enough to keep the house running, there might not be enough to buy it. It must be worth a good deal; its size and its setting alone insured that. So Lord Hazing had been applied to, and had sent nothing but a book. It seemed odd, but the problem was not hers, it was Madame Daumier's.

She had a shower, dressed and went downstairs, no longer in an abstracted mood, but alert and anxious to perform two immediate tasks: to send a telegram to Nigel Frame telling him that she was held up indefinitely, and to telephone to the Splendide to find out whether

Professor Thorwaldsen's memory had returned during the night.

There was no sign of her mother. She wandered into the garden and was greeted by a large white cat. The gardener, as long and lean as his wife was short and stout, worked at a flower bed. Beyond was the neighbouring house, Miramar, which she now knew to be owned by the widower Courbet.

She heard her mother's voice calling to her from an upper window.

"Kerry, good morning. Did you sleep well?"

"Yes, thank you. Would you mind if I used the phone?"

"Of course not."

"And I'd like to send a telegram. Could I do that by phone too?"

"Yes, you can."

A beautiful, diaphanous, pale blue nightgown or negligee. It was hard, very hard not to think of the Aid to Indigent Relatives of the Clergy. It was almost impossible to avoid contrasting this trim garden with the overgrown, unmanageable wilderness that crept closer and closer to Thea's herb garden, or to contrast her mother's soft carpets with her aunts' ragged rugs, or to admire the beautiful china breakfast or dinner sets without remembering the chipped, job-lot assembly that appeared for meals at Orchard House. If she began by making contrasts, she would end by making moral judgments and this she felt not only disinclined but also unable to do.

The telephone call to the Splendide brought nothing but the information that the Professor had gone out. She felt a faint pricking of uneasiness for which she could not account, and reassured herself by the thought that he had doubtless remembered his friend's name and address and gone to visit him.

Then her thoughts went to Nigel Frame.

She stood staring unseeingly at the telephone and faced the realization that it was necessary to tell him more than the fact that she was delayed. Honour, gratitude and esteem combined to convince her that he deserved to be told the whole truth, and the whole truth was that the events of the past twenty-four hours had inexplicably brought her feelings for him into sudden, sharp focus. What she had seen indistinctly was now only too clear: she liked him, but that was all. The trip with him was not only postponed; it would never take place.

She felt sick and shaken at the memory of the months during which she had drifted without being able to come to any decision concerning their future. She had never thought of herself as weak or vacillating, but what else could she label her failure to end the affair instead of allowing it to drag on for so long?

When at last she went into the drawing room, it was with a mind divided between remorse and relief. She found her mother sitting with Nigel Frame's book in her hand, regarding it pensively.

"Did you read any of it?" Kerry asked.

"I couldn't make it out. I thought Bob might have sent it as a sort of joke, but then, he's not the joking kind."

It took a little while for Kerry to identify the label; she knew that Lord Hazing's name was Robert, but she had never dreamed that anybody could think of him as Bob.

"No," she agreed. "He's not the joking kind. Wasn't there anything from him in the post this morning?"

"Nothing."

Madame Daumier, with a slight pout, put the book aside. Kerry looked out through the chinks of the lowered venetian blind at the sea dazzlingly blue. There was a hiss of water from the sprinkler on the lawn in front of the house. A car drove up to the house next door and Kerry caught a glimpse of a chauffeur and a large, stout, bearded gentleman. Monsieur Courbet? She was about to ask, when her mother spoke.

"Wouldn't you think," she asked wistfully, "that a man as rich as Lord Hazing would be glad to help me when I ask him? He promised me that if I ever needed anything, I had only to ask. Well, I did ask."

Kerry studied her thoughtfully.

"What was it that you left behind fifteen years ago? What," she repeated, seeing the incomprehension on her mother's face, "did the message mean? It said you'd refused something. What was it you refused?"

"Oh, I see what you mean. Pearls," said Madame Daumier.

"Pearls?"

"Yes."

"Why did you refuse them?"

"Because I never liked taking expensive jewels from the men I . . . the men I've known. Money, yes, and clothes and small birthday presents or Christmas presents, but when they opened one of those velvet cases and showed me a necklace or a bracelet, I felt . . . I don't know how I felt. I can't explain. I'm not good at explaining."

Kerry did not need any further explanation; the confession revealed only too clearly the creaky clockwork system that operated her mother's mind. No jewels. Everything that looked domestic, wifely, homely, but not an enactment of that theatrical scene: the man, the mistress, the casket of jewels. Was it a refusal to face up to the truth of her situation, her status? Or — fantastic thought! — was it a remnant of Mostyn integrity? Whichever it might be, Kerry felt again the stab of pity she had experienced last night. If ever a woman needed protectors, here was one.

And she had refused the pearls. Lord Hazing couldn't have liked that. She could not imagine him walking meekly back to the jeweler's, case in hand. He was much more likely to —

She gave a sudden gasp, and saw her mother's eyes resting on her in surprise.

"What's the matter, Kerry?"

"Nothing. It was only an idea, and I don't suppose there's anything in it, but I thought —"

She stopped. Footsteps had sounded on the steps outside the front door. There was an imperious clang. Since Clothilde was working in the hall, there was no delay in answering. Kerry thought of Monsieur Courbet and expected to hear the kind of voice that would issue from a heavily whiskered gentleman, but heard instead a young man speaking in a sharp, somewhat arrogant tone. A moment later, Clothilde's knock sounded on the drawing room door, and she entered with a card on a salver. Madame Daumier took it and glanced at it, and Kerry saw her look astonished, then puzzled and at last distinctly uneasy.

There was a pause. Clothilde, waiting orders and receiving none, looked to Kerry for guidance.

"Can she bring in the visitor?"

"The — oh, yes. Yes, I suppose so. Oh, my *goodness* . . ." Madame Daumier murmured in anguished tones.

There was no time for more. A man was ushered into the room. He was very tall and extremely thin — Kerry thought she had never seen anybody thinner — with strong glasses, thick, black, untidy hair and a face that looked as though it had been too hastily put together; a scholar's forehead, a fighter's chin, a woman's sensitive mouth and a nose that had begun by deciding to be Greek and then changed its mind.

95

Why these disparate elements should have combined to make a face as handsome, she could not decide, but in spite of his aggressive expression, she thought him both good-looking and interesting. He looked about thirty. His clothes hung loosely and would have looked better after a thorough pressing. Before Clothilde had closed the door behind her, before Madame Daumier could utter a word, he had broken into rapid French. She put up a hand to halt him.

"Monsieur, do you speak English?"

"Of course. I am sorry, madame. My father told me that your French was not good, but I imagined that after so many years —"

"My daughter, Miss Cromer" — she indicated Kerry, and he gave a brief, impatient bow — "doesn't speak any French. Kerry, this is Pierre Leclair, whose father . . . well, whose father I used to know."

"Speaking in English, I will sometimes falter," he told them. "This is only natural, since I have not spoken English for some time. I have come, madame —"

Once more Madame Daumier made a slight gesture, this time indicating that they should all sit down. He dragged up a chair and sat on it, his manner indicating clearly that he regarded these interruptions as trivial and made simply to annoy him.

"I was saying, madame," he swept on, "why I have come here. You will not, I think, be surprised, but you will perhaps be disappointed.

This is natural. You will perhaps be doubly disappointed, because perhaps you hoped that my father would come."

Madame Daumier stared at him, but said nothing. Her mouth was slightly open, her eyes looked slightly glazed. Kerry felt that she was beginning to recognize this look of her mother's, as well as the bewildered tone in which she began to speak.

"Your father —" she began.

"Please, madame, allow me to go on," he went on. "I have driven a long way. I have come, actually, from Paris, but I had been in the Dordogne and on my return only yesterday evening, I stopped on my way to my studio and visited my parents. It was well that I did so. I found my mother in great distress, almost I might say desolation. At first, she was too upset to tell me what had occurred, and then I learned what it was. You had written to my father."

Having brought out this final sentence in a voice of stern accusation, he paused to hear Madame Daumier's excuses. She merely went on staring.

"You are unmoved, madame. Very well." The ends of his tie fell out and he thrust them impatiently aside. "I will go on. You wrote to my father. My mother saw on the breakfast table this letter to him in your handwriting, which she knows, and she waited for him to give some explanation. But he said nothing, and as he had assured her, assured her faithfully that between him and yourself there was never any communication, she was alarmed and angry. Then she demanded that he explain. He told her that you had written him to tell him that this house was to be sold — this house, Maison du Bois — and that you intended to buy it." He straightened himself in his chair, leaned back and spread his hands wide. "And now, madame, you know why I am here."

There was a long silence, broken at last by Madame Daumier's agitated murmur.

"Oh, *goodness* . . ."

Pierre Leclair, on the point of resuming his monologue, paused and gazed searchingly at her. Kerry saw a look of bewilderment displace the arrogance, and understood why; this could not be the figure he had been expecting to see. Had he perhaps made a mistake? Was this indeed his mother's rival? Peering brought no enlightenment. He spoke again, but with less assurance than formerly.

"Madame, to pretend in this way is childish. You know, you must surely know the reason I am here. It is to tell you, simply, that you cannot buy this house. This is what you wrote to my father that you were going to do. This is why you asked if he would send you money. It is not any wonder that my mother was upset. But this does not affect the matter. What is certain is that you cannot buy the house, as you hoped."

Madame Daumier was roused to speech.

"Your mother never wanted it," she told him.

"She told your father that she'd never come and live in it again. So you see —"

"Are you aware, madame, that she has written year after year to Madame Courbet, to know if she would change her mind and sell it?"

"Yes. Madame Courbet told me. But she said she'd never, never ask me to leave, because I rented it all the year round and your mother only rented it for the summer. And I spent a lot of money keeping it in good repair, but your mother never spent anything and so I had a better claim."

The word made him leap to his feet as though his seat had become too hot to hold him. He looked almost grotesquely loose-jointed. Kerry thought that if somebody stopped manipulating the strings, he would fold up and fall down.

"Claim, madame? Claim? Claim? Are you aware that —" He broke off and turned to Kerry. "You said something, mademoiselle?"

"Yes, I did. It meant sit down and simmer down and don't shout at my mother. If you've anything sensible to say, say it and she'll listen."

He had to wait, she saw with satisfaction, until he could control his rage.

"I am tired of pretense," he said at last. "I do not know how long you have lived in this house, mademoiselle, mees, but you must be aware of what it contains. You cannot pretend, you or your mother, that you are unaware of the considerable reputation I have earned in the world of art. To say that you have not heard of my work would be to show yourselves uncultured, out of touch, and this I do not think you wish to do, and this also I do not believe to be the case. I think, mademoiselle, mees, that I have already made myself clear, but I will make myself clearer. I am here on my mother's behalf to tell Madame Courbet that she is mistaken in supposing that this house can be sold to your mother. I did not know that Madame Courbet was dead; this your mother did not say in her letter. I went first to her house, but they told me she had died and that only her husband was at home. I did not wish to see him, and so I came here to state the position to your mother."

"I don't understand," Kerry said. "Are you trying to say that your mother is making a higher bid for the house?"

"Higher bid, mees?" he said in a high voice. "Higher bid? My mother will certainly pay the price Monsieur Courbet asks, but that is not the claim of which I spoke. If my mother were not able, for financial reasons, to buy this house, do you imagine that it would be allowed to pass into the hands of strangers? Do you imagine that art lovers, art students in France, in England where I worked for so long, in Italy where I studied, in America where in every major city have been exhibitions of my work — do you imagine that they would allow these murals that are here in this house — my first, my earliest painting — do you imagine the house would not be bought, preserved, protected so that people, the public, can come and view? While your mother was here, installed, brought here by my father, renting the house year after year from an owner who refused to sell, nothing could be done. But now it is different. The house is for sale, and as claims were spoken of, I have explained what is the first claim."

He stopped, satisfied at having rounded off his speech with force and point. Turning from Kerry to her mother to see how his words had been received, he saw only a figure apparently frozen — pale, staring, with hands clasped tightly together in her lap.

"You are disappointed, madame," he said. "I am sorry. But there are other houses. It will surely please you, will it not, to know that this house will become a — I do not wish to appear boastful, but certainly it will be a place of pilgrimage. It will be almost, I may say, a shrine."

Once again he stopped. Neither of his listeners made any comment. Madame Daumier had placed her forefingers together and was apparently measuring them to see whether they were the same length. Kerry was watching her mother.

"Do you know what he's talking about?" she asked at last.

Madame Daumier looked up.

"Oh, yes," she said faintly. "Yes, I do."

"I am speaking of my murals," Pierre Leclair said.

"Murals? What murals?" Kerry asked.

101

He gazed at her in surprise.

"You are in this house, mees, for how long I don't know, but you can ask this?"

"I came yesterday."

"For the first time?"

"Yes."

"Even so, you must have seen them. The murals which I painted when I was here in this house as a boy. On the walls of the room in which I slept, which is the room above this one. They were shown by my mother to Charenbert, to Claud Otono, to Zubert; all of them were stunned. They could not believe that I, so young, so as yet untaught, could have painted them. In particular, the one which depicts dawn breaking on the sea — this, they said, was phenomenal. Sensational. So how can this house be sold unless it is sold, as you might say, to the world of art? I do not know how it is that you have not seen the murals. Or perhaps" — he turned to Madame Daumier, his manner for the first time approaching friendliness — "perhaps, madame, you do not allow anybody to use that room, so that my work shall . . ."

Something in her manner made his words die away. He stared at her and then gave a loud cry.

"No!" he shouted. "No! It cannot be that —"

He broke off and in three strides reached the door. Throwing it open, he rushed into the hall and up the stairs. They heard him at the door of Kerry's room. He opened it, and then dead silence fell on the house.

Kerry could only gaze speechlessly at her mother. Madame Daumier met her gaze and spoke falteringly.

"I thought they were t-terrible. Really awful. I could never say so to his father, but I can see now that it would have been better if I had, because —"

She stopped. Slow, heavy footsteps were descending the stairs and crossing the hall. The front door opened and closed — quietly. The wicker gate squeaked. A car engine started, died away and then there was silence.

"He's very angry," Madame Daumier said unnecessarily. "If I'd asked his father about them, he would have explained that they weren't really so awful. When he went away, I brought my own furniture from Paris, and Madame Courbet allowed me to redecorate, and she didn't say a word about the murals and I thought she'd be glad to have them cleaned off her walls."

"But . . . dawn breaking on the sea?"

"That was red streaks, and blue streaks below, stretching from your dressing table to the little writing desk. It looked like smoke coming out of a chimney, only there was no chimney. On the other wall, the wall behind your bed, there were nude figures, very large and rather — Well, I thought that perhaps he was going through one of those stages they say boys go through."

"And his father never spoke about them?"

"No. He said his son might turn out to be a good artist, but he'd rather he followed in his footsteps and took up music, because he was a very good violinist, or perhaps it was the cello he was good at. No, it was the violin."

"When he left and went back to his wife, didn't he mention the murals?"

"No."

"Doesn't that make it seem as though Madame Leclair didn't have any special feeling about them until her son became famous and she remembered them?"

"But his mother, didn't he say she showed them to all those people?"

"He didn't say they'd come especially to see them. Albert Leclair came here every year, and donated a hostel somewhere near here. They probably came to visit him, and while they were here, his wife took them upstairs to show them the murals."

She was speaking to comfort, but she began to see that no comfort was needed; the subject had lost its interest for her mother, who was looking pensive and recalling the past.

"He isn't in the least like his father," she said reminiscently. "Albert was extremely good-looking. Women simply flocked to his concerts, just to see him. I met him at a reception and I didn't speak more than three words to him, but I couldn't forget him, and then he got in touch with me and — well, it ended by our coming down here together. We were very happy. It was only when he began to feel that his son needed him that he decided to go back to Paris. He knew that I'd never be able to lead his life, going from country to country. Why did he, Pierre, I mean, say that Monsieur Courbet was at home? I didn't know he was back."

"If he's large and bearded, he's back. I saw him arrive in a car."

"A green car, with a chauffeur?"

"Yes."

"Then he *is* back, and he'll want to know about the rest of the money, and I haven't got it. I suppose he'll wait. He's got to wait. I want to stay here. I fell in love with this house the moment I saw it, even when it had terrible furniture, and now I've made it beautiful. Don't you think it's beautiful?"

"Yes. Did you ask Albert Leclair for money? That is, did you ask him for half and Lord Hazing for the other half?"

"I just said that the house was for sale and — what's the matter?"

Kerry had picked up the book that Lord Hazing had sent and was staring at it, her gaze curiously intent.

"I had an idea just before Pierre I-am-a-genius walked in," she said slowly. "Now it's more than an idea. Got a knife?"

"A *knife?*"

"Knife. Penknife. Anything."

Madame Daumier, puzzled, opened a desk and handed her a small, silver-handled paper knife. Then, seeing the use to which it was to be put, she gave a cry of protest.

"Kerry, no! Not that beautiful binding!"

Kerry had already inserted the knife under one end of the book's spine. Taking a deep breath, she slit the leather and then, putting down the knife, tilted the book and shook it gently above the table. Onto the marquetry surface rolled a succession of small, perfectly matched pearls.

For some time, there was no sound in the room. One of the pearls rolled toward the table edge, and Madame Daumier put out a hand and stopped it. She picked it up and replaced it gently among its fellows. Then she lifted her head slowly and looked at Kerry.

"We were both wrong," Kerry said calmly. "After all, he is the joking kind." Her calm splintered into fury. "Blast him."

"You're angry!" her mother said in amazement.

"Angry? Of course I'm angry. 'Take the book,' he said. 'Don't put it down for a single instant,' he said. And I didn't. And if the customs or the *douane* had thought of inspecting it, where would I be now? I'd be in the Bastille, that's where — and a fat lot he'd care."

"Kerry, I'm so sorry. But you must admit that it was a generous gesture."

"Who ever accused him of being mean? And this time, he's been really lavish. You got them both."

"Both?"

"Your daughter and your ducats," Kerry said, and walked out of the room to escape the sheer hard labour of trying to make her mother understand.

Chapter Five

The beach was not crowded when Kerry walked down to it after lunch. At the point where each zigzag path from the houses ended in the sand where four pink-and-white striped tents marked with the names of the houses to which they belonged. She spread her towel in front of the canvas Maison du Bois, slipped out of the beach robe she had borrowed from her mother, arranged the beach cushions in a pile and then lay with her head on them, an arm shading her eyes from a too-warm sun. She counted a dozen adults and about twenty children. The harbour looked like paintings she had seen in the windows of art shops. Among the motor yachts was a newcomer, large and white, looking like a toy liner. She thought it probably belonged to the summer visitors at the Villa Gabrielle, who had arrived noisily as she was leaving her mother's house. The tenants of the fourth house, Clothilde said, were expected later in the day; that completed the hillside population. They would stay until the winds grew chilly, and then they would go away — all except her mother and Monsieur Courbet, who would stay here and be company for one another. If peace was what you wanted, here it certainly was. You could live here for years without opening a newspaper or worrying about how the world was faring. No news. No politics. No commentators. If anything sensational happened anywhere, the tradesman would tell Clothilde and she would tell Madame. That was what they called getting away from it all.

The gaps in her mother's life, she reflected, were being filled. There was her father for one. There was Lord Hazing. There was Albert Leclair. Nobody could really accuse Madame Daumier of being grasping; all she appeared to have been left with, after those years of association with rich men, was some furniture. She had loved them and left them, and it was a comfort to feel that she had not stopped to fill her pockets as she went. But to fill her pockets she would have had to be shrewd, and to be shrewd she had to be calculating, and to calculate, you needed a brain.

These musings were interrupted by a small, plump, pretty woman in her thirties who paused beside Kerry, gave her a searching look and then, with a satisfied smile, settled down beside her. From a capacious bag she brought out swimming suits, pails, shovels, packets of sweets, inflatable arm bands and a vast packet of paper tissues.

"You don't mind if I stay here, do you?" she asked Kerry in the voice of America. "The others look kind of foreign, and if there's one thing I can't do, even after ten years living here in France, it's get along with people speaking a foreign language. You'd imagine, wouldn't you, that by this time I'd — Priss!" She raised her voice to a piercing shriek. "Priss! Come here like I told you and put these arm bands on before you go near that water."

Priss, aged about eight, was in sand shoes and a bright red bikini. Her platinum-fair hair was drawn up to the top of her head and tied in a bunch, the ends falling over and looking like a miniature palm tree. She approached, giving a realistic imitation of a steam engine, her feet scuffing up sand and sending a shower over her mother and Kerry.

"Look what you've done! Just look, Priss. All over me and this lady. How often have I said to you to watch yourself? Now put these on."

There was a silent interval as mother and daughter blew energetically into the mouth-pieces of the arm bands.

"There. Now listen, Priss. If they get loose, you come right back here and show me, and I'll tighten them up. You know what your father said, you can't go in unless you've got them on."

"Aw, why?" snarled Priss. "Why me, and not them?"

Kerry looked apprehensively toward Them and saw two boys, one about Priss's age, very thin and small, the other about ten, large and in her view far too fat.

"They can swim, that's why. Now you go tell Jumbo I want him. I didn't tell you my name," the woman continued, turning to Kerry. "We're called Drummond. We're from Phoenix, Arizona, at least my husband is, and that's where I was living when we got married, but he's got this engineering business, Drummond's, and he's been over here in France, on and off, ever since he was thirty, running it. Sometimes I come over with the children, and sometimes I go back home and stay with my mother-in-law, because she's kind of old and she likes to have the kids around, and then when it gets too much for her, we come back here. Only sometimes we come back just as my husband's taking off to fix a job in this or that place, and I'm stuck with the kids in Paris, of all places. We got here this morning, on that yacht, but this is a vacation."

Kerry wondered how long they intended to remain ashore. There was something appealing about Mrs. Drummond, but she was clearly a compulsive conversationalist. Going for a swim would be a way of escape, but nobody could stay in the water indefinitely.

"Are you visiting?" Mrs. Drummond inquired. "You didn't tell me your name."

"Cromer. Kerry Cromer. I'm staying with my mother."

"Is she French?"

"No. English." Kerry smiled at the frank questions. Mrs. Drummond had hair as naturally fair as her daughter's, and a tanned, blunt, schoolgirl's face. She was wearing a sleeveless jacket patterned in violent blues and greens, and shorts to match. Her legs were brown and bare, and bronze sandals dangled from her toes.

"I wouldn't have said this was a place a pretty girl like you could have a good time in," she remarked. "Not on this beach, anyway. The other beach is kind of gayer but once you get these kids where they're selling anything to eat, they — Jumbo!" she shrieked without warning, and at a pitch that sent a tremor through Kerry. "Jumbo! Didn't you hear Priss telling you I wanted you to come here?"

To Kerry's surprise, it was not the fat boy who approached, but the thin, undersized one.

"Everybody thinks Jumbo's Pete," his mother explained. "But he isn't. Pete's the big one. How it happened was, you never in all your life saw a baby as big as Jumbo, and that's why we named him. He's Matthew, really, but Jumbo stuck, and I guess we'll never get to calling him anything else."

Jumbo, for all his lack of inches, looked formidable. His natural expression seemed to be one compounded of suspicion and ferocity.

"Whajjer want?" he demanded of his mother.

"You didn't take your glucose sweets. How d'you expect to get to be a big boy if you don't do —"

"Aw, gimme!" He snatched the packet, ignored his mother's angry protests and leaped away to rejoin his brother and sister. As he reached them, Priss grasped the packet and dodged out of his way. His yells, her yells, Pete's yells rose and filled the air. Their mother shrieked admonitions, and when these had no effect, seemed about to rise and join the scrimmage — but this proved unnecessary. Jumbo, unaided, punched Priss on the nose, almost uprooted the palm tree and then, taking a few steps backward, gave a running jump that ended with his head against Pete's ample stomach. Pete went down and a few seconds later Priss went down too, with Jumbo on top of her, burying her face in the sand.

"They never learn," their mother said resignedly. "You'd think they'd know by now that Jumbo's a real tiger. There isn't a gang in his school that's not scared of him. If you leave him alone, he's all right. I guess if you're undersized, like him, Nature makes you kind of aggressive. His psychiatrist says he — Will you just look what he's doing now?"

Kerry had been looking for some time. A French boy, obviously anti-American, had put his foot on Jumbo's sand castle. Jumbo had retaliated by turning him upside down and was busy punching his head. The scandalized French family — father, mother and sisters — intervened, rescued the victim and bore him away.

"I don't interfere unless I have to," Mrs. Drummond explained. "People know they can't take it out on Jumbo, so they take it out on me. His psychiatrist, he's more a friend really, says to let him be. Jumbo's father doesn't agree with that, but then he doesn't have to have Jumbo around all the time, like I do. That's one of the things I don't like about men, the way they come in nice and fresh from the office and start telling you how you should have managed the kids all day. And Sundays, the Sundays when my husband's around, that is, they behave themselves, and he says that proves I don't do it right. They're good at putting you in the wrong, men are. Look at the way I said it was crazy to take a trip on a yacht because the kids would fall overboard, and my husband said they wouldn't, and they didn't."

Kerry thought this a great pity. It was becoming obvious that if she wanted to regain the peace she had been enjoying before the arrival of the Drummonds, she would have to remove herself.

"We'd got all fixed up to go on vacation to Switzerland," Mrs. Drummond told her. "And then what should happen but suddenly Ben — that's my husband — comes home and says we're not going to Switzerland at all, we're going to take a nice trip on a yacht. Of all things, for heaven's sake, why a yacht, I said to him. With three kids all guaranteed to take a running jump over the side, why a yacht? But Ben had met this man who had this yacht for hire at St. Malo, and next thing, he'd hired it, just like that. You know, I had a kind of funny feeling when he came home and told me — you know how you get a funny feeling sometimes, with men? I had a funny feeling there was more to it than just an innocent trip. He's good-looking, Ben is, and when I'm around to see what he's up to, I see. But I can't be around all the time, and when I'm not, I try to act philosophical, like his mother told me to do, and not stay awake trying to figure out what's behind it. We've only been married ten years, but he's all of fifty-five. I'm not his first wife, but I'm the only one he's stayed with. We get along fine, and when I get suspicious, like now, and think maybe he's playing snakes without the ladders, I just string along, and I don't let the string go, either. You ever been married? Well, even if you haven't, an attractive girl like you must have learned something about men, so you —"

She stopped. Pandemonium had broken loose again. Priss had appropriated Jumbo's pail. He had waited until she returned with it from an expedition to the water's edge, and then he emptied it over her head and rammed the pail down over her nose. With sand and seawater streaming down her face, pail-blinded, she was being led by Pete toward their mother. Jumbo was placidly digging.

Under cover of the confusion, Kerry rose and walked down to the sea. The water was colder than she had anticipated. She went in a little way, dived and then forgot everything in the pleasure of moving swiftly through the water, arms and legs moving rhythmically, head turned at regular intervals for breath. She swam out for some distance, made a swift somersault turn and retraced her course at top speed.

Later, treading water, she watched events on shore. The Drummond family seemed to have split up; Mother had Pete and Priss, while Jumbo had been joined by Father. Studying the tall, well-made figure, Kerry thought that his wife might possibly have some reason to hold on to the string; fifty-five or not, his body in the dark green trunks looked hard and fit; his hair was just gray enough to give distinction to his handsome, clean-shaven face. Even playing games with his small son, he gave her the impression that there was a side to him that was less than paternal. The impression deepened when she saw that he was watching her and that he was strolling casually to the point at which she would leave the water.

He bent to pick up a shell; that, she judged, would furnish him with an approach and reassure his wife.

Yes, here it came. His eyes, narrow, shrewd, gray, smiling, rested on her. His voice was deep and attractive, but the gambit, she considered, was disappointingly hackneyed.

"Haven't we met somewhere before?"

"No."

The monosyllable was not as chilly as she usually managed to make it in similar situations, and she was not surprised to find it insufficient as a rebuff. He held out the shell.

"Look. Broken," he said. "Step on that, and you'd be left with only one foot." He turned and fell into step beside her. "My wife told me you'd made friends. But you were sitting near one of those tents with a name on it — Maison du Bois.

Doesn't that mean it belongs to the house up on the hill?"

"Yes."

"That's what I thought. If I told you I had a special reason for asking if you were staying at the house, would you overlook the impertinence?"

"I'm staying with my mother. She lives there."

Perhaps it was her imagination, but she felt certain that her words checked something he was about to say. Perhaps he didn't follow up approaches with girls who were staying with their mothers. But it was hardly that. His eyes, coming to rest on hers for a moment, had had a startled look. Whether she would have learned why, she did not know, but the approach of his wife put an end to the exchange.

"I see you two've met," Mrs. Drummond said as she joined them. "Ben, her name's Kerry Cromer and I don't see why we shouldn't try and persuade her to come aboard the battle cruiser and have a drink."

"Would you?" her husband asked Kerry who, warming despite herself at the smile, the touch of eagerness, the glance of appeal, wonderful nevertheless how much of it came from natural charm and how much from years of practice.

"I'd love to some time — if I'm here long enough," she said.

"And don't think," Mrs. Drummond detained her to add, "don't think you'll have the kids pestering you. When we ask our friends over, we pay

116

someone to keep the kids where they belong. How about tomorrow?"

Kerry tried to be evasive, but Jumbo, standing by with his brother and sister, fixed her with an unwinking stare that she knew penetrated disguises.

"Aw I bet you won't come," he diagnosed.

"Really? How much?" Kerry asked him coldly.

"Two bucks; two bits; what's the difference?" he answered.

"Two bucks *and* two bits," she told him and walked away. For two bucks and two bits he'd probably put poison into her glass. What was it like to be a Jumbo and fight the whole world? What he needed was an infusion of Mostyn blood to turn him into a peace lover.

She neared the tent, and with intense annoyance saw that someone had taken the place vacated by Mrs. Drummond. It was not a large beach, she admitted, but there were wide areas of empty sand, why choose a place so near somebody else?

Then she identified the figure sitting hunched up on an inadequate towel. Pierre Leclair.

He made no sign of recognition; he seemed lost in gloomy meditation. His arms were clasped round his knees; as he wore only bathing trunks, she could see that the knees were as bony as the rest of him. He had used the tent to change in; she could see his clothes lying untidily inside, and her annoyance increased.

She shook out her hair, dried herself, spread

the towel on the sand and sat down on it. Pierre Leclair continued to gaze out to sea, silent and brooding. Then suddenly he spoke without preamble and without turning his head.

"I do not understand," he said. "It is impossible to make myself understand. I have been trying to think clearly, but I am still puzzled." He turned to look at her. "Do you know," he demanded, "what my father said to me about your mother? No. How can you know? You were not there. So I will tell you. But before I tell you, I wish you to understand that my father is a clever man. A brilliant man. A man of education, of culture. And he, this man of education and culture, said to me that your mother had been, for a time, his inspiration. Can you believe that he should say a thing like that, about a woman like your mother? Do —"

"Yes. I —"

"Please allow me to finish what I am saying."

"You asked me a question. I was answering it."

"It did not need to be answered. It was a — I do not remember the word which means that a question does not need to be answered. I was only asking myself. When I came here to Gaston-le-Grand, to speak with your mother, I had formed a picture of her in my mind, copied from a word-picture that my father had painted. As well as saying that she had been his inspiration, he said — and this is what is so strange, so incredible — he said that when he was here, with her, he did his best work. It is true that during those years he did the Bazerline arrangements and orchestrations, and it is for those works that he will be remembered, so much must be admitted. But to say that it was because of her, to say that she was always helpful, never demanding, never jarring, always fitting into his every mood — it is this that I cannot believe. But when he said it, he believed it. He was speaking seriously, speaking at the time not just after he had returned to my mother, but much later, when I was older, when we had become more intimate. He has never said that my mother inspired him — and yet my mother is educated, cultured like himself, sympathetic, understanding the demands of his profession and keeping his domestic life calm. I do not wish to offend you, but to know my mother, and then to meet yours, is to wonder what spell my father fell into. If you take away your mother's beauty, which I will admit she has, what will you have left? If I said that she is lifeless, wooden, even shallow, certainly unresponsive, you would be angry; but in what other way can you describe her?"

There was a pause.

"Is that another rhetorical question?" Kerry asked.

"It is certainly difficult for you to answer."

"No, it isn't. If there hadn't been something lacking in your mother, why would your father have gone looking for it somewhere else?"

"The only lack, the only possible thing missing was this fairness, this in a way ethereal beauty.

But my father was capable of seeing more than a mere surface. He liked women, sometimes he even loved a woman, but always a woman of distinction, of wit, of charm. So naturally I imagined, I assumed your mother to have these qualities, and what did I find?"

"You've been into that. My opinion is that if my mother'd been brimming over with wit and charm and distinction, you would have written her off because she hadn't appreciated your murals."

"That is all you care," he said bitterly. "You do not blame her. You do not believe that she destroyed a work of genius."

"Is that what you are, or were?"

"I am not speaking in a personal way. I am only saving that for a boy so young, only fifteen, to have produced such mature, such finished, such original work, that might be called genius. You do not have to be bearded before you can claim merit as an artist. Perhaps you have never heard of Mozart, of Menuhin, of Michelangelo. You are going to say that these were prodigies. I was not. I wished only to point out that genius can — can manifest itself at an early age. You do not have to enter for examinations and obtain diplomas proving that at eight, at ten, at twelve you were exceptionally gifted. People, discerning people, discriminating people see your work, and at once recognize its quality."

"Why blame my mother? If you thought, or if discerning and discriminating people thought so highly of your work, why, when you knew the house was being rented by —"

"Do you think that was the only work I did at that time? The only murals? Do you know something? In the lycee, today, the classroom in which I studied, and where at the request of my master I painted murals, this is now — you know what?"

"A shrine. A place of pilgrimage."

"Certainly. If you are sneering, you show yourself to be lacking in education, in culture. You —"

"Look," she broke in impatiently, "why waste all this ammunition on my mother, and on me? Why don't you go home and attack your father? He was in the house when you painted those murals. They were left here when he left my mother and returned to yours. So why didn't he —"

"You think he wished to encourage me in my painting? No. You do not know what you are saying, and I cannot blame you for that, because you do not know that always, always, always he dreamed of me to follow him as a musician. I had gifts, great gifts in both branches, but he wished to see me like himself: a musician, famous. He saw, he could not help seeing that I was a gifted painter, a promising painter, but sometimes promise is not fulfilled. In music, he could guide me, be of use in —"

"Yes, but —"

"— my future career. In painting, he could only be an onlooker. How do you know that this did not make an influence when he went away from this house? Why should he say: these murals must at all cost be preserved, because one day my son will be a famous painter? How could he —"

"Yes, but —"

"Why do you interrupt, mees? You ask me something, I try to make a reply, and you break in. You wished to know why my father said nothing about the murals. Perhaps that is why: because he was sure he could persuade me to —"

"Yes, but —"

"Once again," he pointed out angrily, "you prevent me from finishing what I wish to say. This is very impolite, mees."

"Would you please stop addressing me as *mees?* My name is Cromer."

"Yes, I remember. That is what your mother told me. Crrromer. Then, Miss Cromer, I — where are you going?"

She was gathering her towel and robe and was on the point of rising.

"Back to the house," she said. "It's quieter."

"Quieter? Here on the beach there is no crowd and — ah, you mean to say that you do not wish me to speak to you? Very well. I understand. It is because I have been frank when I have spoken of your mother. I think that you agree with me, but you do not think you should admit it. But please wait. There is something I wish to ask you."

"Well?"

"It is this. Perhaps you will refuse, but all the same it is a good idea. This is what the idea is: I shall teach you French, as —"

122

"Teach me French! How long do you suppose —"

"Kindly wait until I have made my explanation. I shall teach you French, because when I came, your mother said that you did not know any. This seems extraordinary to me, because I would have thought that every person of education would be able to conduct at least a simple conversation in a language so beautiful, so widely studied. But I will teach you, as much as possible, because I am not here for long. In return, you will teach me how to swim."

"You can't swim?" she asked, astounded.

"What is so surprising?"

"You came here year after year, you lived a stone's throw away from this beach, you —"

"Some boys are athletic, some not. I was not. I did not wish to enter the water. My mother and my father did not like to swim. Now I should like to learn from you, because I watched you when you were in the sea and I saw that you were very expert. In these few days, will you teach me?"

"I thought you rushed down to Gaston-le-Grand solely to prevent my mother from buying the house."

"That is correct. But three friends of mine are at present staying in the hostel — the hostel my father gave — and today a fourth is coming, and they are going to practice a string quartet which one of them has composed. I would like to hear the work, and so I am going to stay for a few days. But not at the hostel, because that is not allowed

123

except for work or for rest, and I am not doing this. So I have got a room at the hotel."

"The Splendide?"

"Yes."

"You haven't by any chance seen an old gentleman there, have you?"

"I have seen three, no, four old gentlemen. Which one is your friend?"

"Well, he's —" She broke off. "It doesn't matter."

"How long are you going to stay with your mother?"

"I don't know."

"Where do you live?"

"In London."

"With your aunts?"

"How on earth did you know anything about my aunts?"

"I know nothing about them. I know only that your mother told my father, during their association, that she had two daughters who were being brought up by some aunts. These are in London?"

"No. They live in the country. I work in London and live in a flat."

"Alone?"

"Yes. My sister's married."

"I did not mean your sister. Do you often visit your mother? I mean — since you told me you are here for the first time — does she often visit you?"

"No. Aren't you supposed to be teaching me French?"

124

"The swimming lesson shall come first, and then, while we are getting dry, we shall speak French. Come."

He rose, lank, unbelievably bony, bespectacled. His trunks, maroon-coloured, were too large, and he had bunched them to keep them up. On his chest was a forest of black hair, against which his skin looked bleached. He put out a hand to pull her to her feet, and they walked down to the water. Scarecrow he might be, she thought, but there was something in his manner that was authoritative, even compelling. Why else was she embarking on this ludicrous mission?

She stopped at the sea's edge.

"Your glasses," she said. "Take them off and go and put them with your clothes."

"*My glasses?*" He sounded thunderstruck. "Take off my *glasses?*"

"Of course."

"But no. Not at all. You do not understand, mees — Mees Cromer. Without my glasses, I see almost nothing, or at least only a little way. I shall meet with something."

"What, for instance? A tanker?"

"A boat, another person swimming, perhaps a rock. If I am swimming, and soon I shall swim well, I must know *where* I am swimming — to the ocean, or to the shore."

"What's the use of glasses all covered with salt-water?"

"I shall not put my head underneath the water

125

today. Only at the following lessons."

"If I'm going to teach you to swim — and now that you've got me so annoyed, I'm going to make a real job of it — then you're going underneath the water, head and tail and teeth. Take off those glasses."

"The responsibility will be yours, mees."

"Save your breath for swimming. Take off those glasses."

He took them off, and ten years fell from him. His eyes, large and dark and defenseless, peered helplessly down at her. Watching him place his glasses on a scooped-up pile of sand, she felt remorse, and hardened her heart. He was grown-up and he wanted to learn to swim and it was high time he did. Lesson One.

When the water was lapping at his knees, he hesitated.

"We shall begin here," he said. "Here I can —"

"Come *on*."

When the level of the water had risen to his chest, she was out of her depth, paddling easily beside him. The waves, gentle enough, were beginning to exert more pressure than they had done near the shore. She took his hand, and he turned his blind look on her.

"Now listen," she said firmly. "Turn yourself away from me and let yourself down slowly. I'll get hold of your shoulders and support you, and when I do, you can take your feet off the bottom and float and get the feel of the water."

He obeyed her meekly. She gripped his shoulders, found them slippery and attempted to widen her hold so as to support him by the arms. As she was changing her grip, he stretched out his legs. She clutched at him, missed, and saw him sink like a stone.

She plunged, realizing through rapidly mounting panic that she had somehow to get her hands under his body and lever him up. His legs and arms were thrashing wildly, but he was on his back and she saw no way of lifting him. With strength born of terror, she gave a tremendous push and managed to turn him onto his side. His own convulsive efforts did the rest. To her infinite relief, she saw first his head and then his shoulders appearing above the water.

For the next few moments, she could only thump his back and listen to his chokes and splutters. His hair hung like a black mask over his forehead and eyes. With his first deep breath, he put up his hands and pushed it back and stood staring down at her.

"I swam!" he croaked in triumph. "I swam! Did you see me? I swam!"

"Swam? You sank!"

"You said that I must go underneath. That is what I did. But you are not a good teacher, because you did not give me enough warning that I must go underneath on my stomach and not on my back. What shall I do next?"

"Find another coach."

"Coach?"

She made an impatient sound.

"Never mind. Now listen."

She taught him the rudimentary arm and leg movements. She supported his chin while he made efforts to keep above the water. He sank, reappeared, choked and tried again. His lips and his nails turned blue, his teeth chattered.

"Out," she commanded at last.

"Why? I am not tired."

"You're frozen. You've had enough."

"Only a little frozen. I will get used to it. Shall I know soon how to dive?"

"I said *Out*."

He followed her, trying to protest but prevented from doing so by the spasmodic working of his jaw. When they reached the tent, she picked up his towel and threw it at him.

"Get that round you," she said. "And then lie down and let the hot sand do the rest. You're not built for swimming; you haven't got any protective blubber."

He wrapped the inadequate towel around him and sat beside her, shivering. Angry, anxious, she waited for him to stop shaking.

"Get up and do some jumping," she suggested after a time. "That'll get your blood moving."

He obeyed. After the second leap, his trunks, which in the water had clung to him, showed a disposition to descend. He clutched them firmly.

"I shall go and put on my clothes," he said.

He went into the tent, and she sat brooding on the strange new weaknesses that had seized her since she left England. She would have said that the one quality she shared with her aunts was that of detachment, of mind-your-own-business, of total uninvolvement. So why should she be feeling uneasy and restless because an old man had lost the address of a friend? Why harbour this odd spark of pity for her mother, who appeared to have everything she wanted in the world? And here it was again, a feeling of protectiveness welling up for this bony stranger in the tent behind her, so thin that she was surprised he wasn't rattling as he drew on his clothes. Why should her mind be filled with all the fattening articles she had excluded from her diet — porridge and pastry and potatoes, suet pudding dripping with hot jam, batter puddings glistening in hot gravy, thick, milky chocolate, trifles piled high with chopped nuts and whipped cream? What was he to do with her? What had his educated and cultivated mother been doing all these years? Only one child to look after, and she had allowed him to grow like a beanstalk, all in one direction.

He emerged from the tent and sat down beside her, and she saw that he had stopped shivering.

"Next lesson, I shall propel myself," he prophesied. "You will be surprised at how much I will improve. And now we shall begin your French lessons. You know, of course, about nouns, verbs, so on?"

"Not much."

"At school, they didn't teach you?"

"At school, I didn't pay attention."

"How much can you say in French?"

"*Je ne peux* —"

He closed his eyes in anguish.

"Terrible. Oh, terrible," he moaned.

"Well, go ahead and make it better. Don't just sit there looking sick; tell me what was wrong."

"Everything. This is not school, so perhaps you will pay attention. Please watch my lips. Do not say *per,* as you did. That is not French. *Peux.*"

"*Peux.*"

"No. Not at all. The *sound* is wrong. Where is your ear?"

"There's one on each side. Take your choice."

"It is of no use to be angry. Say after me: *Peux Peux Peux.*"

"*Peux. Peux. Peux.*"

"*Je-ne-peux-pas.*"

"*Je-ne-peux-pas.*"

"*Peux. Eux. Oeuf.*"

"*Peux. Eux. Oeuf.*"

The lesson proceeded. She would have liked more vocabulary and a good deal less pronunciation, but she was prepared to believe that this might be the wrong approach. There was no point in uttering even the few words she knew if the people to whom she addressed them closed their eyes and made agonized faces.

He was not pleased when she said at last that so much *peux, oeuf* and *eu, eu, eu, eu, eu, eu* had given her paralysis of the jaw. He allowed her to rest, and they sat watching the children playing nearby.

"Those other children, who came from the *Jolie Demoiselle*, have gone," he said with relief. "One was a devil. The little one. But brave; very brave."

"What's the *Jolie Demoiselle*? That yacht?"

"Yes. I know her well. I know her owner. He lives in Paris, and keeps the yacht at St. Malo for hire, at such a price that only rich Americans can pay it."

"These are Americans."

He nodded.

"This is what I thought. Do you like children?"

"Some children."

"In Paris, I have a choir of children, from the ages of six to ten."

"So young?" she asked in surprise.

"That is what everybody says: so young? Yes, so young. I do not continue when they have learned to sing together properly. What I do, I simply assemble them and divide them into groups, and I give each group a note and make them sing it, and soon they find they are singing a splendid chord, and this they like very much — singing in harmony. I astonish their parents. But this is easy, to astonish parents. They do nothing to foster their children's talents, and then when someone else discovers them, they say: Oh, really? Can he or she really sing, or play the piano, or dance?"

"Some parents, perhaps. Not your parents."

"No, not my parents." He glanced at her. "You are making a joke?"

"I'm stating a fact. Didn't you say they knew straight away what a genius you were?"

"And so you find this a joke? What is funny?"

"Nothing's funny. Claiming genius, even if you've got it —"

"Ah! I must pretend? Must I say, as when people are asked if they play tennis, bridge, golf, that no, I am unable, even if this is not true? This is not modesty, you know, mees. It is simply false. What you can do, you may claim to do. Is this wrong?"

"It's likely to be inaccurate. How many people can judge their own performance? Ten minutes ago, you claimed to be able to swim. If your talent as a painter is as outstanding as your talent for swimming, then I oughtn't to have worried so much about my mother's removal of your murals."

"When you have children, if you have not already, you will do well to encourage them, as my parents encouraged me."

"When I have children, and I have not already, I shall try to judge their merits impartially. What makes you take me for an unmarried mother? Do you think it runs in families?"

"No, I do not. Why do you get angry all the time? You like to speak frankly yourself, but you do not like to hear others saying what is true. You may joke about my parents, but I may not mention your mother without making you resent what I am saying. This is not reasonable. How can I help knowing who and what your mother is? She has been in my life, you might say, since I was fifteen years old. And shall I tell you something else? I do not find you truthful, because you told me that your mother did not often visit you, but when I was dressing in my tent, I remembered that my father had told me that she said she had not seen her children since they were infants. So one of you, she or you —"

"Me. She told the truth."

"Then when you came here, to Gaston-le-Grand, you —"

"You'll find this hard to swallow, but it's true. I was sent here with a message to her. I had no idea who she was until I walked in and recognized her. I knew her because she's the image of my sister. She knew me because I'm as like my father."

He stared at her in amazement.

"This is really true? Yes, I think it is, because you are serious. When you saw each other, you were moved?"

"If we'd been French, I daresay we'd have   "

"This is not for joking. When my father told me this, I said she had abandoned you, and he was shocked that I thought this. He said there must have been good reasons for her to take this difficult decision. But I did not change my mind, and so I will go on to say that this is what she did, and as this is so, I may claim to know much more about her than you, because I can tell you, mees — this mees, mees, mees is becoming very stupid."

"I said so, didn't I?"

"Why can't I say Kayree?"

"You can, if you'll try to get the pronunciation right."

"Kerry — Kayree . . . Kerr-y. If I were you, I would not accept that your mother will stay always in this house. She is not old, she has still her good looks; even if she does not wish to leave, someone will persuade her. When the summer is over, the two other houses will be closed, and there will only remain your mother and old Monsieur Courbet, and she will get tired of him because he is foolish, and he will not make a good protector because he is even more an old woman than he is an old man. His wife was rich, and she looked after him like a child. If you will believe this, she called him Tom-Tom and he called her Pussy. Naturally he would wish your mother to buy the house; if she left, he would be alone all winter. He was always no doubt your mother's admirer, and only Pussy prevented him from being more."

"My mother comes from a family that finds everything it wants within the home. My aunts —"

"Perhaps your aunts do not look like your mother. But whether she stays or whether she goes, she will be quite all right, because foolish people have sometimes a gift for looking after themselves. My only surprise, when I learned that she had written to my father for money, was that she had had to reach backward to the past; I would have thought that there was no need of this, for I am quite certain that she has not been unprotected for the past eight years, since my father went back to my mother. To think so is to be naïve. There is another thing. If she appealed to my father, then she must also have written to other men from the past, and if they have not wives or sons to protect them, they will wish to answer in person, as my father would have liked to do, if I had not prevented him. He could not come, but how do you know that other men to whom she wrote will not find their way back to her? You will see that — Now you are angry again."

"No. No, it isn't that." Kerry was staring at him with a strangely blank expression. "It isn't that. You've just made me think . . ." She got to her feet in a swift movement and began to gather her things together. He rose and helped her, his face puzzled and uneasy.

"I have said something to offend you?"

"No. I've just thought of something terribly important. I'm sorry. Goodbye."

She raced up the steps and across the road. She took the zigzag path in bounds, opened the wicker gate and left it swinging. The front door was unlocked. She went to the drawing room, opened the door and to her intense relief saw her mother.

"There was something —" she began, and then stopped to regain her breath and also to regain control of herself. She waited until she could speak calmly. Madame Daumier, behind a silver-laden tea tray, said nothing, but looked apprehensive.

"I wanted to ask you something," Kerry said at last. "When you heard this house was for sale, you wrote to Lord Hazing, didn't you?"

"Yes. You know I did, Kerry."

"You wrote to Pierre's father, too."

"Yes. Why are you asking?"

"Because it suddenly occurred to me that you might have written to . . . to some others, too."

Madame Daumier picked up the teapot and put it down again.

"Well —" she began.

"Did you?"

"Well, yes. Yes, I did." The admission came reluctantly.

"How many?" Kerry inquired.

"I — as a matter of fact, I wrote to four people."

"Four men?"

"Yes."

"Asking them for money to help you buy this house?"

"Well, I explained how it was that —"

"Yes. I know two of the men. Would you tell me who the other two were?"

There was a long pause.

"What I did was choose four men I knew were very rich and wouldn't miss the money. If there'd been time, I would have written to them one at a time, to see if they'd help me. But Monsieur Courbet —"

"Yes. You told me." Kerry did her best to keep impatience and irritation out of her voice. "Did you ask them to come here?"

"Come here!" There was genuine horror in the cry. "Come here? Oh goodness, Kerry no! When you told me that Lord Hazing had actually thought of coming, I —"

"Pierre's father thought of coming too. If those two did, I wondered if —" She paused to swallow the distaste and fear raised by the thought. "I just wanted to know if I could expect my father to arrive and —"

"No."

The tone was sharper than any she had heard her mother use, and it carried complete conviction. Relief flowed through Kerry, a relief that seemed to shake her. The idea, she saw, had been as unwelcome to her mother as it had been to her.

"Is that what was worrying you?" Madame Daumier asked.

"That, and something else. Would you mind telling me who the other two men were?"

The answer came slowly and unwillingly.

"One was an American."

"Called?"

"Benjamin Drummond."

"He —"

Kerry bit back the words. Benjamin Drummond was out there on the yacht riding at anchor in the harbour, and his wife had been right to sense something suspicious in his sudden dash to Gaston-le-Grand. But the Benjamin Drummonds needed no protection. They could look after themselves.

"Who was the fourth?" she asked.

"The fourth?"

"The fourth man you wrote to. He couldn't be a Dane could he?"

He couldn't — could he? — be a perplexed professor groping for a name that had eluded him?

Her mother was looking at her in panic. She had risen and her hands were clasping her cheeks.

"Kerry, you — you mean he's — he's here?"

"I travelled from Paris with a Dane. A professor of languages. He —"

"Tall and thin? With wavy, fair hair, sort of silvery at the temples? Blue eyes and a rather boyish face?" babbled Madame Daumier in agitation.

The answer in all cases was in the negative. The wavy hair and the boyish face had undergone certain changes, but Kerry had no doubt of his identity.

"I won't see him," Madame Daumier spoke with finality. "Kerry, I won't see him. He must be crazy, after twenty years, to — where is he?"

"At the hotel."

"Go and tell him I'm away, please! Tell him I don't live here, that I've left, been called away or . . . or something. Anything. Please, Kerry! Don't say anything to hurt his feelings; just make certain that he goes away. Oh, please hurry! How do you know he isn't on his way to this house at this moment? Please do this for me. Will you?"

"Yes," Kerry said unhesitatingly, and heard her mother's gasp of relief. Yes, she would certainly do it. She would go and see him. What she would say when she came face to face with him, she did not know, but she would not let him come here to be rebuffed and hurt. "Yes, I'll go. I'll have to dress first."

"I'll order the car," Madame Daumier said.

Kerry turned in surprise from the door.

"Car? I didn't know you had —"

"Monsieur Courbet lets me use his whenever I want to. Oh Kerry, hurry!"

Kerry closed the door behind her.

Chapter Six

The chauffeur drove the car around from the small, flower-covered building next door that Kerry had taken to be a summer house. She was driven round the curve of the hill; the pinewoods were left behind and the town came into view, looking, in contrast with the green seclusion she had found at her mother's house, even more seedy than it had on her arrival. But she was not thinking of Gaston-le-Grand. Her mind was full of Professor Thorwaldsen, and as she neared the hotel, she found herself divided between doubt as to his still being there and uncertainty as to what she would say to him if he were.

There had been no sign of Pierre Leclair when they had driven past the beach, nor did they pass him on the way to the hotel. But as she was struggling to make herself understood at the reception counter, he came through the revolving door and, seeing her, paused in surprise.

"I'm sorry I left you so abruptly," she said. "It was —"

"It was to come here?"

"No. Yes. Can you tell me what this man is saying?"

Pierre, inquiring, informed her that the man wished to know what she had been saying.

"I asked him if there was a gentleman here called Professor Thorwaldsen. He said there was, after which I couldn't follow anything else he told me."

"He informed you," Pierre said, after a further exchange, "that the Professor had gone out."

"That's all they ever said when I phoned, that he'd gone out. Will you ask if he had any friends here?"

"Yes," the florid, fatherly receptionist told them. "The Professor had one, but on his arrival, having a bad memory, he had temporarily forgotten the name and address."

"Yes, I know that," Kerry said impatiently. "So what —"

"Yesterday and today," said Pierre, "it appears that the Professor walked about in the town to see if any of the street names refreshed his memory. But they didn't. Then this afternoon, when he had rested, he came down and told this man that he had fortunately remembered the name of his friend, a lady. He —"

At this point the receptionist, who had been straining to follow the thread of the conversation, broke in to tell them, and to illustrate with a vividness that brought the Professor clearly before Kerry, the happy outcome of the incident.

"The Professor told him the lady's name, and he knew it and was able to supply the address," Pierre translated. "So the Professor went to visit her."

Kerry stared at him.

"He went to . . . to see her?"

"Yes."

"When?"

Pierre put the question to the man.

"He left the hotel about half an hour ago."

"Did he walk?" Kerry asked.

"Yes. Do you want to wait here until he comes back?"

"No. I mean — no, thank you. I'll go back to the house."

"How did you come here?" Pierre inquired.

"In Monsieur Courbet's car. I sent it back."

"Then I will take you back in mine. It is not a very good car to look at, but perhaps you will not mind."

After a moment's thought, she decided to accept the offer. There was a hope — faint, but enough to give a spark of reassurance — that she might get to the Maison du Bois before the Professor. It was some distance, and the last mile was a stiff climb. She might be in time — in time for what? she wondered. Perhaps in time to save him from being hurt or humiliated. He would ask for Madame Daumier and she would refuse to see him.

"If you're sure you don't mind," she began, but Pierre was already at the revolving door, waiting to lead her out to the car. It was, as he had stated, not good to look at. It was an aged two-seater, hoodless, high-slung and battle scarred. He put her in and walked to his place at the wheel, and they started with a jerk that came near to dislocating Kerry's neck.

"Thorwaldsen," he shouted above the engine's clatter. "Is he perhaps the African-languages Thorwaldsen?"

She nodded. They turned off the busy street on to a narrower but clearer one, and after another series of jerks, the noise of the engine dropped to an angry growl over which normal tones could be heard.

"Do you know him?" she asked.

"No. He is well known. I have heard of him. He is a friend of yours?"

"No. He travelled on the same plane, and then on the same train, and he got very upset when he lost the address. I advised him to go to the hotel, and I went there just now to find out whether he'd remembered it."

"And he has remembered it, and now all is well for him, but you are still worried. Why is this? You are sorry that he has found the address?"

"Of course I'm not," she said irritably. "But nobody likes to find themselves in a strange town without any idea of what they're doing there. But —"

"But in a way, you wish that he had not remembered?"

Whether she would have replied, and what she would have said, she could never afterward remember. They had driven past a small, tree-shaded square and she had seen something that made her clutch Pierre's arm and address him in an urgent voice.

143

"Stop! Oh, please stop!"

He stopped the car abruptly. She twisted around on her seat and stared in the direction from which they had come. Then she began to struggle with the door handle.

"Wait, wait, wait," Pierre said in a soothing tone. "There is no need for such agitation. I will open the door for you."

He came round and opened it and she half-stepped, half-fell out.

"Thank you. Please don't wait for me," she said hurriedly. "I've seen the Professor. It was very kind of you to drive me here. Goodbye."

She doubted whether he heard the last words, for she was going as fast as she could toward the corner, her mind full of the disturbing sight she had seen. It had certainly been the Professor — but why here, why looking like that, why . . .

She turned the corner. She had not been mistaken. On a bench in the dappled shade sat Professor Thorwaldsen. His shoulders sagged. He was holding, listlessly, a large spray of flowers. His eyes were fixed unseeingly on the ground.

Her first thought was that he was ill. He had set off eagerly from the hotel, the excitement had been too much for him, he had become exhausted and had sunk onto the first available seat.

She reached him at a run. Behind the row of benches was a rail-enclosed area of parched, neglected grass. All around the square were houses, small, double-storied drab. The only passersby

144

were two children, an errand boy and a woman carrying a baby.

"Professor!"

He looked up, and for a painful moment she thought that he had been weeping. Then he blinked, frowned and made a tired attempt to rise.

"Stay where you are," she commanded, and sat down beside him. "What are you doing here?"

He did not answer. He was patting her hand gently, as though to assure himself that she was really there. He was murmuring her name.

"Miss Cromer. Ah. Miss Cromer. I am very, very glad to see you. You cannot know how glad. I did not know —" He paused uncertainly, as though he had lost the thread of what he was saying — "I did not know you were still in this place."

"I thought I was going away at once, but I didn't. Will you please tell me what you're doing in this square, on this bench? Are you feeling ill?"

"Ill? Oh, no, no, no; I am not ill," he assured her. "I am only tired." He gave a long, heavy sigh. "Or I shall say the truth to you, because you are so kind. I am sitting here, Miss Cromer, because in the past half-hour I have understood something that I have never properly realized before. I am an old man." His words dragged. "I am a very old, old man."

"Rubbish," Kerry said angrily. "You're hale and hearty and you're only one day older than you were yesterday."

145

"No. That is not true. I am much, much older than I was yesterday. Yesterday, I was under illusions. Yesterday, I thought to myself that I was — oh, not young, but certainly not as old as my total of years told me. Today, I am my age. I am an old man."

"You simply feel that way because you've been silly enough to come out on a hot afternoon, walking instead of taking a taxi. I'll go and fetch one and —"

"Please!" At the desperate appeal in his voice, she gave up any idea of leaving him. "Please do not leave yet. I am almost myself. I have recovered almost fully. It is just that I have — I have had a shock."

Then he had already been to the Maison du Bois, she thought with a sinking heart. He had been turned away. But why had he not left the flowers? Why —

"You have been very kind to me," she heard him saying. "I have never before met any young girl so kind. If you will allow me, I will tell you why I am sitting here, and then you will know all the story — why I came, and why it was a mistake to come, and why I know that I am a foolish old man."

"You'd feel quite different," she told him gently, "if you'd let me take you somewhere cool, where you could get a drink and rest until you felt stronger. You'll soon be all right."

"I am all right now, Miss Cromer." He managed to smile. "I am myself. You see, I remembered —"

"I know. I went to the hotel to see you. The man said you'd remembered the name of the lady you came here to see."

"Yes, I remembered. At first, I telephoned to the bank. They knew nothing of my wallet. I should then have gone away at once, gone home, bowed to what I now think was the working of fate. I should have told myself that I was not meant to make this visit. But instead, I stayed. I was sure that I would recall something. This town is not pleasing, but it is healthy; I felt confident, rested. I walked about a little, here and there, thinking that perhaps there would be the name of an avenue or a house that would remind me. But there was nothing until this afternoon, when I was able to go to the man in the hotel and announce that I had remembered, if not the address, at least the name of my friend. And to my great relief, he told me at once that he knew this lady and could give me her address. He wrote it down." The Professor opened his clenched fist and disclosed a crushed piece of paper. "Look."

Kerry took it, smoothed it and read what was written on it.

Madame Dubois
15. Place de la Republique

She stared at it, unable to speak. The Professor resumed his tale.

"Yes, Miss Cromer, it was a lady I had come to see. When I knew her many, many years ago, she

147

had another name. This is why I was so agitated when I forgot her new one. When it came back to me, when the man supplied the address, I cannot tell you how I felt. Happy? Oh, much more than that. I was excited, because I once loved this lady. I said to you that it was a long time ago, but I can tell you that it was on a June day, almost like this June day, but eighteen years ago, that I met her and fell in love with her. So when she wrote to me suddenly, from this past, I lost my head and I decided that I would come myself in answer to her letter. And so I came."

He paused. Two small boys passed, pushing a third in a homemade wooden cart, their shouts almost drowning the squeaking of the wheels. A man walking with a little girl stopped and swooped her up onto his shoulders. Somebody in one of the houses pulled down a sun blind.

"I came to this address," the Professor continued. "Number fifteen. It is that house you see over there, near the end, the one with the green door. I brought flowers. I walked, to give myself time to compose myself, to think what I would say. After so long, it is not easy. I reached the square. I looked at the numbers —"

He broke off, staring unseeingly at Kerry. She waited.

"I came almost to the right number," he went on after a time. "And then the green door, the door of number fifteen opened and — and a woman came out. She was well dressed. She — yes, she was handsome. But she — she —"

This time she was not mistaken. His eyes were full of tears. Kerry, in an agony of pity and embarrassment, watched him fumbling for a handkerchief and tried desperately to decide whether to explain that he had made a terrible mistake and must come at once to her mother's house, or whether it was better to let the affair die in this shabby square. Here, or at the Maison du Bois, what was the difference? she wondered miserably. Either way, he was certain of heartache and humiliation. She leaned over and took the flowers from him.

"Thank you. Thank you. I am foolish, no?" he murmured. "But some lessons are hard to learn. You see, Miss Cromer, she was the same, and yet not the same. She was not an older version of the person I had loved. I expected, because I am not a fool, that she would be changed; this I had prepared for. Hair: this would be perhaps gray, or white. Cheeks: these would be lined or wrinkled. Figure: perhaps even this, once so beautiful, would be ruined by time. This would make no difference to me, I thought. Beneath the changes, I would see and recognize the woman I had loved. You see, Miss Cromer, how absurd, how ludicrous, how unforgivable this is in a man of my age, a man like myself? When I think how you must regard me, I blush for shame."

"You needn't." She found it difficult to speak. "You needn't. People change. People —"

"Change? Oh, yes. This everybody knows. This, every wise person prepares for. But if I may

149

in some measure justify myself, I should like to tell you a little more of this history which has such a sad ending. Will you have the patience to listen?"

"Yes."

"It was in Paris that it began. I had been travelling, just as I was travelling when I met you. But in those days, I did not forget everything. In those days, I did not need my daughter to look after me, as now. I had been giving lectures in New York, and I had to stop for business in Paris on my way home to Copenhagen. I was very tired, and I wished to be quiet and undisturbed, so I found for myself a small hotel near a little square like this one in which we are sitting now, but much more pretty, much, much more pleasant. There was a bench near some flower beds, and I used to sit on it, and nobody else came and I was glad. Then a lady came and also sat on the bench, and after a little while, I couldn't help seeing that she, like myself, wished to be away from crowded places, even perhaps wished to rest, like me. She was rather small, and fair — very fair — and beautiful. Also, she was quiet and gentle. There was no real beginning to our friendship; we did not smile, we did not speak. For the four days that I stayed in the hotel, we saw each other in the square, parting when mealtimes came, meeting again when they were over. Only on the last evening did we begin to speak with one another. I told her that I was going to Copenhagen. She told me the name of her hotel and we agreed that when I came back to Paris, we should meet, dine together. And this we did. I saw her several times. Then I went to lecture in Oslo, but we wrote to each other, and when the lectures were finished, I returned to Paris — to join her. I was a widower. My wife had been dead many years; my daughter, our only child, was teaching in a school in Switzerland. I asked my beautiful friend to marry me, but she refused, because she said that my life was spent in travelling, and she wished above all things for a permanent home. But she came with me to Rome and to London and to San Francisco, and we rented, in between these travels, an apartment in Paris. I knew that such happiness could not last, and of course, it did not; after two years, we had to go our different ways. But I never forgot her. I have never met any woman who demanded less for herself. It was not a case of self-denial; I mean simply that she seemed to have none of the usual feminine craving for dress, for trinkets, for baubles. She bought what she needed, sensibly, without fuss. I do not think she had many domestic talents, for most of our time together was spent in hotels. But she had something — I cannot express it — a sense of one's mood. She knew, instinctively, like a natural musician, the right accompaniment. She was herself always, but it was a self that seemed to adapt itself to the nature of the person she was with. She did not make any effort to please; she simply adjusted herself effortlessly, unconsciously, to my needs. She was as natural to oneself as the clothes which one wears day by day. One chooses the ones necessary for this climate, for that function; one puts them on and they are right. Being with her was like that. In the two years she was with me, I did my best, my most lasting work. When at last she went away, I could not feel sad, because to look back was to remember only happiness." He gave Kerry a faltering smile. "So you see, Miss Cromer, it would have been better for me if I had not come back to the past, here in Gaston-le-Grand. A happy book should not have a sad ending. It has been sad only because an old man did not like to admit his own foolishness, and also because in coming back, I found a woman not only changed by the marks of time, but a woman whose very nature had changed. This I did not expect. But now I know that people may grow old in many ways, and she had grown old in the wrong way. She was once gracious and gentle; now, no more. She —"

"You spoke to her?"

"Spoke to her?" He shuddered. "No, I did not."

"Then how do you know for certain that —"

"— that it was she? As she came out of the house, I was approaching from one side. A man, an acquaintance of hers, drew near from the other. He called her name, Madame Dubois. It was quite clear. She turned to wait for him; then they walked together toward me, she saw me, an old man standing aside to make way for her to pass. There was no recognition, there was no interest. There was only a desire to please her companion, a manner forced, arch, ugly. They passed me, and when I had recovered a little, I came to sit down on this bench. I had to adjust myself. I had to agree at last with this other man inside me, who since I left my home has been telling me that I am an old fool, trying to recover something which had gone forever. Keep your memories, that other man said. But I didn't listen, and now I should be sorry, but I am glad, because —"

He stopped abruptly. Over Kerry's shoulder, he had seen something or someone. A look between fear and distaste showed on his face. Half-turning from her, he hunched himself like someone anxious not to be recognized.

The click of heels on the road told Kerry what to expect. The Professor had now twisted himself around on the bench and was gazing fixedly at the withered grass behind them. Her eyes went to the woman who was approaching. And at sight of her, some extraordinary, inexplicable, totally unexpected filial instinct sprang to life within her and brought the angry blood to her cheeks. How could anyone dare to imagine that her mother could ever look like this? How could the Professor, who had known and loved her mother, believe that she had turned into this brassy creature? She wanted to drag him to the Maison du Bois and confront him with the form he had come so far to find, to punish him for his lack of faith and vision.

But with her eyes fixed on the woman who was now passing the bench, with her eyes on her until she had reached and entered the green door, she realized that the Professor had had some justification for his error. The age was right: middle forties. Stoutness: that could happen to anyone. Still-slim ankles. Black-and-white outfit, smart, a shade too smart. A golden wig, cheeks dabbed with rouge, and the hard, hungry expression of a cat on the prowl, but with something, nevertheless, of lost beauty and grace.

Fate, she knew, played strange tricks, but Kerry thought this one particularly mean. The Professor had come on a romantic errand and had got nothing for his trouble. He had lost his tender memories, he had wasted his time and his money and he had learned that it would have been better to have stayed at home. But this was better, she reflected, than to have arrived at her mother's door and been turned away.

The Professor had turned to face her. He spoke with resentment for the first time in his tone.

"She did not tell me the truth," he said. "That, more than anything else, makes me able to be myself again. She did not tell the truth. Since I have told you so much, I can tell you that she wrote to me to tell me that she wanted to buy this house, and would like me to send her some money. She said that it was the settled home she had always wanted. She said that it was beautiful, in a pinewood overlooking the sea and therefore expensive, too expensive for her to afford. And so I came — this is my crowning folly — I came here to buy it for her. You see how foolish an old man can become, Miss Cromer? But it is finished, and now there is nothing but to return to my daughter, to my home, to my work, and forget that I ever came to Gaston-le-Grand. But even this has some compensation, because I met you, and I hope that one day my daughter will also be able to meet you."

They sat in silence. Kerry held the dying flowers and found nothing adequate to say. She did not know how long it was before she touched the old man gently on the arm and suggested returning to the hotel.

When they reached the corner of the square she found, with a rush of gratitude, that Pierre Leclair's car still stood beside the pavement. In it, immobile, patience itself, sat Pierre. Seeing them, he got out and walked to meet them, and after brief introductions, the Professor made his wishes clear: he would like to return as soon as possible to Paris. Perhaps Pierre could find out for him the time of the first train that would enable him to reach Nantes to connect with the Paris plane?

He sat between them in the car. Kerry waited in the hotel lounge while the two men went upstairs and returned with the Professor's luggage. They drove him to the station, and with each kilometer, the Professor shed the miseries of the past hour and became the vague but untroubled passenger who had taken the seat beside Kerry in Paris. There was a little confusion about return tickets, which he thought had been left behind at the hotel but which were discovered in the lining of his hat. Seated at last in the train his only words, besides those he spoke in gratitude, referred to his daughter. She would be glad to see him, and he would be glad to place himself once more under her wing.

He leaned out of the window until the train went out of sight. Kerry, turning away, gave a sigh that held regret, pity and also a measure of relief.

"Is it a secret," Pierre asked, as they walked out to the car, "why the Professor bought expensive flowers and went to sit on a bench?"

"Not a secret. Just a misfortune. He came here to see someone he'd known years ago. When he saw her again, he didn't like her, that's all."

"Ah. That is all."

"No. And it's not quite true, either."

"This I know. I am not so stupid. We were sitting together on the beach, you and I, and I talked of men who might come to see your mother because she had written to them, and at once you grew pale and ran away and went to seek out an old professor, and you found him on a bench and you had tears on your cheeks when you returned to my car, and now the Professor has gone home. So much I could see for myself. And the rest I can guess, because —"

156

He stopped. A high voice had addressed him imperiously.

"I say, you!"

Parked behind his car was one so small that it looked like a toy. On the pavement beside it rested the largest trunk Kerry had seen since her schooldays. Two porters were attempting to explain to the tall, spare, elderly owner that a trunk of that size would not fit onto the luggage rack of a car so small. She was listening impatiently, and turned once more to summon Pierre.

"Come over here a minute, will you? Heard you speaking English with a French accent. Explain to these johnnies, will you, that if I say that trunk will fit on the roof, that trunk will fit on the roof. Silly race, the French. Slow, too; that trunk's been three weeks doing the same journey that I did in my car in three days. Now come along, young man, say something to these men. Something strong. They've no business to argue. That trunk's been up on my car roof from one end of England to the other, many and many a time. Ginger them up, will you?"

Kerry, standing discreetly aside, gazed at her. Long-faced, tweed-clad, with thin ankles and long feet and long, well-kept hands. There wouldn't be many more of these sharp-tongued, arrogant, well-bred, devastatingly rude types, once so well known in country lanes and Continental resorts. Goodbye for ever, and a good thing too, she mused.

The trunk was being hoisted up. It settled on

157

the roof and the porters stood open-mouthed, expectant, waiting for the roof to cave in.

"There you are, you see? A lot of fuss for nothing."

Pierre was not looking at her. He was studying the label on the trunk, and as the woman paid the porters, he read it aloud.

"General Arran-Duff. Villa Azul. Gaston-le-Grand. I could have taken the trunk in my car," he said. "I know the house."

"Then perhaps you know the General. I'm his sister, Miss Arran-Duff. Tell these porters to go away, will you?"

"You have not paid them enough," Pierre told her.

"Ah-ha! Now *that's* where you're wrong, my good young man. I went to the trouble of borrowing a printed, official list of prices. Here it is." She produced it and waved it at him. "You see? *Fiacres, pourboires,* all the —"

"It may be printed and official," Pierre told her, "but it is also outdated."

"I can't help that. I shall use it while I'm in France," declared Miss Arran-Duff. "Where did you say you lived?"

"I said only that I know the Villa Azul and could have taken the trunk there for you."

"Not a bit of it," declared Miss Arran-Duff. "I'm not going to let any of my luggage appear there before I do. This is a surprise visit. For seven years, the General has rented this place, and I've waited in vain to be invited. Now I've in-

158

vited myself, and I'm not going to have you giving the show away by going up there with my trunk. I shall take it myself. They told me I'd never get here driving on the wrong side of the road for the first time in my life, but here I am, safe and sound. It just shows you."

"The porters are waiting to be paid," Pierre reminded her.

"Take no notice. Mind out of the way, will you? I want to get off and see my brother's face when I turn up."

"Aren't you going to put a rope around the trunk, at least?"

"Rope? What for? Haven't I just explained that I've taken it just like that, unroped, from Land's End to John o' Groats and it's never rolled off yet. You see? Those men have gone. They try to swindle you, and if you let yourself be involved in a brawl, you're done. It's the same in England, all grossly overpaid. Like these porters. Ignore them, and they get tired and go away."

"I should perhaps translate for you what they said about you as they went?"

"Oh, that? My good young man, one gets used to that. Well, goodbye."

She got into the car, started the engine, made a wide turn, proceeded for some distance on the wrong side of the road, came almost nose to nose with a cyclist, leaned out to shout at him and then changed to the correct side.

"Mean old stinker," Kerry said dispassionately. "When you see people like that, you wonder how it is they've been allowed to live so long. If you'll find those two porters for me, I'll pay them a bit more and retrieve England's honour."

"A kind thought, but it would be an injudicious action." Pierre looked at his watch. "Are you in a hurry to go back to your mother's house?"

"No. Especially now that the Arran-Duff is so near. Why?"

"Because I would like to visit the Villa Leclair — the hostel. I want to listen to the string quartet; they will practice it this evening. It is to be performed for the first time in Paris next month. Would you like to come and hear it?"

"Well . . ."

"You don't like music?"

"I'm not too strong on string quartets."

"What would you like instead?"

"A full orchestra, with extra cymbals and drums. Bits of harp solo running up and down, all nice and liquid. A concerto, with the soloist shaking hands with the conductor at the end, to deafening applause. A nice, gay first movement, a dreamy bit in the middle and a —"

"A finale with extra cymbals and drums?"

"Yes. Crash, crash, boom — CRASH."

"I am sorry. I have only a string quartet to offer. Two violins, a viola, a cello. It has — you are not paying attention."

"I'm sorry. I just thought of something you said on the beach this afternoon."

"About music?"

160

"No. About my mother."

He opened the car door and waited for her to get in.

"If I were you," he said, "I wouldn't worry about this until you have seen the General."

"How did you know I was thinking about the General?"

"What are you likely to be thinking about? An old woman who underpays porters? This is not interesting. A string quartet? You have said you do not like them. Your mother, and what I said on the beach, that it would be naïve to imagine that she had lived here for the past eight years, ever since my father went back to Paris, without what we shall call protection? That is what you were thinking about, isn't it?"

"Yes."

"But to clear up a puzzle, you must have all the pieces, you must know all the clues. At present, you know only that the General is here and that he does not invite his sister, perhaps does not invite other friends or relations. This you will find out, perhaps. But I think you may be sure that the General will not look, will not behave, like his sister. He will, I think, be upset when his sister drives up with her big trunk on her little car. But if she interferes with his plans, it will not be so serious for your mother. Instead of the General, there will be Monsieur Courbet to amuse her. And now that this is cleared up, shall we go and listen to the string quartet?"

She got into the car.

161

Chapter Seven

The car seemed to be skirting the town. They had left the last little shops behind, and the streets had widened until they had become tree-bordered avenues with houses standing in lonely dignity behind impressive iron gates. There were no longer passersby to stare disparagingly at the shabby car, though these had not worried Kerry. If she had ever been self-conscious, she thought that her girlhood excursions with her aunts would have cured her; Elvira's man-size boots, Thea's gardening hat, Sylvia's fur tippet, Dulcie's truncheon, carried to repel mad dogs who might bite or Englishmen who might rape — these had all but stopped the traffic on many occasions in High Green, and Kerry and Dale had grown indifferent to stares.

"I thought this hostel was in Gaston-le-Grand," she said to Pierre. "Where are we going?"

"The hostel," he answered, "was given by my father for the purpose of providing solitude and peace. Should this be in the middle of a town?"

It proved to be in the middle of a field, a large, ugly, spreading house with nothing around it but meadow on which cows grazed. They approached it by a wide, rutted road flanked by poplars. Kerry could see distant chimneys but no other houses. Beside the front door stood a farm cart, its horse unharnessed and tethered to a tree. It raised its head as the car approached and then went on contentedly cropping grass. This scrunching was the only sound to be heard when the car's engine stopped.

"You see? Peace and quiet," Pierre said. "Here they can work without disturbance."

"Can anybody come and live here for nothing?"

"Anybody, no. Only my father's pupils or those who were once his pupils. They come mostly from Paris; most are poor and cannot have a room set apart where they can work, or practice, or compose. At my father's school in Paris there are of course practice rooms, but for certain hours only. Here they may come and live for any period up to a year."

"Who looks after them?"

He stared in astonishment.

"Who — do you mean who wakes them up in the morning with their breakfast, who cooks, who washes, who irons, who —"

"Yes, that's just what I did mean. If you're composing, you can't be cooking, can you?"

"If you are composing — and this I know well, because I have composed, first a sonata for violin and piano, then a —"

"You don't eat, is that what you're going to say?"

"I have noticed this many times before," he told her angrily, "that you do not wait to hear the

163

end of what someone is going to say."

"You're always going off the subject," she complained. "I ask about domestic help, and you go off at a tangent giving me a list of your wonderful compositions. Then —"

"Did I say that they were wonderful? This is distinctly a false impression of what I said." His spectacles flashed at her in fury. "And to expect footmen, butlers, here in a place like this hostel, this is absurd, ludicrous. I think you are sometimes unintelligent, or perhaps you only pretend this in order to make others angry."

They were still sitting in the car; it seemed as good a place as any in which to quarrel.

"Let's begin again," she suggested, but not amicably. "This house is for budding composers, right?"

"And for musicians. And for painters. For artists, artists, artists."

"Don't shout. This house is for artists, artists, artists. They can come here and live quietly, without paying. But they have to eat, haven't they? Or are they too busy to bother?"

"They eat, certainly. There is a telephone. Beside the telephone there is a list of shops. They order things. They do not order beefsteaks, because they are poor. They order milk, bread, eggs, bacon, sausages, fruit, cheese, butter — these things. The food is brought out to them from the town, and when they are hungry, they eat. But they eat only things which do not require much cooking, only instantly, like bacon or omelettes."

"I see. How about hot water and baths?"

"There is a well. If you look, you can see it over there. There is a handle. There is a bucket. They go to the well, they pump the handle, they draw up the bucket. What more?"

"Washing, ironing? Clean sheets?"

"They bring bedrolls. They sleep on these. In winter, they make a big fire and they are warm. I will tell you, since you do not seem to know these things, that what an artist needs above all else, when he is working, is to be left alone. When he is hungry, he will be obliged to feed himself — impatiently, absently, his mind anxious only to continue what he was doing. He does not require every three hours a servant to bring a tray. He will manage for himself."

"He won't stop to wash up, of course."

"No, he will not. And so there will be dirty plates. He will not dust or sweep, and so the house will get dirty. He will not notice. I would not notice. Nobody who knows the soul of an artist will expect anything else. I hope that no man who is an artist will ever be your husband, because — this I can see plainly — you will drive him from his senses. You will knock on his door and say, 'Come, eat,' or, 'Dinner is getting cold,' or 'Please wipe your shoes,' or, 'Why do you not take notice of me, of the children, of our friends?' How many wives," he demanded passionately, thumping the area of tattered leather seat between them, "how many wives have I not seen, wives of my friends, my friends who were artists,

165

great artists, driven crazy by these wives who —"

"Yes, you've said all that. Dinner's on the table, and so on. See what I mean about going off the subject? The subject was housework. You've admitted that the plates and the floor and the house all get dirty. So who cleans them?"

"A woman comes."

"Why couldn't you have said so before? Which woman? One of the wives?"

"There are no wives here. These are students only, young men and women who have as yet no wives and no husbands. If you look over there, you will see chimneys. They are the chimneys of a farmhouse. From there, the farmer's wife comes every morning to clean the house, to put things into their places. It is her husband's cart that you see there; he lends it for going to the station, coming from the station. He also —"

He stopped. From the house had come the first sounds they had heard since their arrival. Somebody was playing swift, brilliantly executed arpeggios on a violin. Pierre clambered hastily over the door on his side, took a few paces toward the house, remembered Kerry and came back.

"Please come." He spoke impatiently. "They are beginning."

As he spoke, the violinist was joined by three other members of the quartet. Without further ceremony, Pierre turned the large brass knob of the front door and went inside. Kerry, following him slowly, found herself in a large hall. Beyond it she saw another large room and beyond that a kitchen. All the furniture was of the type chosen for hard wear — solid, leather-covered chairs, rag rugs worn almost to shreds, large tables covered with baize. There were no curtains.

The door of a room on her right opened, letting out the sound of the music. Pierre looked out and beckoned. She followed him in and sat on the stool he placed for her near the door; the quartet, oblivious, went on playing. All four, she saw, were young — three men and a girl, the men bearded and unshaven, the girl with long, straight, stringy hair and a thin, intent face.

The movement ended. Kerry was presented without ceremony to Leonic, Hans, Henri and Bernard, and another movement began and she knew that she was forgotten.

She sat listening and did her best to understand the music, but it had no discernible theme and nothing that she thought of as harmony. In her view, which she admitted was limited, music could only be called music when it chose a key and, after no matter how much wandering, returned at last, like the cows at eventide, to the place from which it had started out. Watching with awe and admiration the bony elbow of Leonie working like a piston, Hans's fingers curling with incredible rapidity and agility along his viola strings, she thought that all four players looked as though they needed a few weeks in the sunshine. But you couldn't, she mused, be out in the sunshine and on your music stool too. You couldn't be both artist and athlete. You were either a doer or a dreamer. These people were creators, while the other kind — her kind — were concerned only with knocking seconds off the world's fastest times. Time was nothing to the artist, everything to the athlete. Who could dream if he was pounding along the four-hundred-meter stretch?

She looked at her watch. She had been sitting there for twenty-five minutes. The music had been interrupted now and then by the sharp tap of Bernard's bow against his music stand. They had paused, peered at the music, tried it over again one by one and then all together, they had used the pencils kept on the music stand to mark this or that passage. They had consulted Pierre, who twice had seized Leonie's bow and violin and dashed off a few bars to show them his own interpretation. Hans had argued, he and Pierre had shouted, then they had all shouted, and after that they had proceeded with the rest of the music.

After another ten minutes, Kerry got up and wandered into the kitchen and stood looking about her. When the first impression of disorder had passed, she saw that there was tidiness of a sort. The plates, though unwashed, were neatly stacked; the stores, some wrapped, some open, lay in a line on a shelf. Perishable food was covered by an enormous mesh mushroom, and the bluebottles, though noisy, could do no more than crawl on the outside. By the sink stood three large buckets of water. In a wall cupboard with a mesh front she saw a variety of sausages and so many different kinds of cheese that she counted them and made the total twelve. There was bread by the yard and eggs by the basketful.

In the hall was a telephone and beside it, under the list of shopkeepers, the list of Gaston-le-Grand subscribers. She found her mother's number, with some difficulty got through and then explained that she was delayed and would not be back in time for dinner.

"Kerry, did you see Christian?"

"The Professor? Yes. He went back to Paris."

"Was he — did he seem hurt?"

"Yes, at first. He decided that it had been a mistake to come. He was feeling better when he left."

Why, she wondered, didn't she tell the true story? She knew that she would never tell her mother more than she had told her in those brief sentences. And yet he was, or had been, her mother's concern; she herself had nothing to do with that old association.

"Where are you speaking from, Kerry?"

"The musician's hostel. I came here to listen to a new quartet. Pierre brought me."

"If you get caught up —"

"I know. I won't get any dinner. But I've found some food. If they go on practicing for much longer, I'll help myself."

Wandering back to the kitchen, she tried to imagine how her mother had fitted into this mu-

169

sical world. Had she ever sat on a hard stool and listened to four people who sounded as though their music had been inadvertently mixed up and they were playing four different works? It was hard to believe. It was easier to picture her at the Maison du Bois, pretty, at ease, awaiting the return of Albert.

The kitchen was occupied. Two young men, one clean-shaven, one bearded, looked around at her in surprise as she entered. She did not need to be told that they had been painting, for they were at the sink removing stains from their fingers. With her scanty French and their scantier English they managed to make conversation. They learned that she was hungry and invited her to join them at supper. They washed plates and opened a bottle of wine while she cooked omelettes, sliced sausages and bread and put them on the table.

"You come 'ere wiz Pierre?" the bearded man asked. His name was Claud; his companion was called Georges. They became gay over the meal, corrected her mistakes in grammar, commended the omelettes and helped her to make some more. They opened more wine, and she was in the middle of learning a song entitled "Mimi-ma-Mimi-ma-mie" when the door opened and the four members of the quartet entered, followed by Pierre.

"You are here, eating?" he said in surprise to Kerry.

"Yes. I was hungry. I would have come and

told you that there was a meal ready, but I remembered what you said about artists not eating."

He was examining the contents of the cupboards.

"What is left for us?" he inquired hopefully.

At midnight, they were still sitting around the table. The plates were stacked high, the empty wine bottles were lined up in front of Georges. Someone, at some time, had lit a fire in the adjacent room and there had been a suggestion of moving in there, but nobody had moved, and the fire had gone out. It was when Georges opened another bottle of wine that Leonie remembered that she and Hans were due in Paris on the following morning to attend a rehearsal of the orchestra to which both of them belonged.

The realization brought panic. Everyone shouted except Kerry, who could only understand one word in ten, and on whom the wine had had a somnolent effect. Pierre was shouting more loudly than anybody else, and she saw him in the hall, looking for and at last locating a railway timetable. No, there was no time to go in the cart, he shouted up the stairs to Leonie and Hans, who were packing. No, there was no time to go in the cart, he yelled to Henri and Bernard, who had harnessed the horse to the cart. Only if they took his car could they hope to get to the station in time.

All four members of the quartet scrambled into it. The bedrolls fell out and Hans got out to retrieve them. Kerry stood at the front door watching the car as it bumped and lurched over the ruts, turned onto the main road and went out of sight. Silence fell, broken only by the clink of metal as the horse, impatient to be off, tossed his head and pawed the ground. A half-moon appeared from behind the clouds and as suddenly vanished, leaving only the dim circle of light that shone from the front door.

She went inside to look for Pierre. Like the horse, she wanted to go home. She wondered how long it would be before the car returned.

She heard excited voices on the upper floor. Going up and walking along an uncarpeted corridor, she stopped at the open door of a room in which stood two easels. On these were works that Pierre was inspecting, making suggestions that the two artists shouted down. None of them took any notice of Kerry, and after a glance at the canvases, she thought it wise to withdraw before her opinion of their merits was asked for. If there were still people who thought that pictures should tell a story or that music should send listeners away humming a tuneful snatch, they ought to be sent, she thought, to the Villa Leclair.

She went downstairs and curled up on one of the big leather chairs. She awoke half an hour later to hear sounds in the kitchen. Investigating, she found Pierre with the two artists, eating bread and cheese.

"So you woke up at last," Pierre said through a

mouthful. "If you are hungry —"

"No, I'm not."

"There is hot coffee."

"Well, yes. Thank you. But it's nearly half past one."

He nodded, and put bread and cheese and coffee before her.

"When you are ready, we shall go," he said.

When they had finished, he said goodbye to the others and led Kerry outside. The sky was cloudless, the moon shone.

"But — where's the car?" she asked.

"Obviously, they did what I said. If you miss the train, I said to them, then you must drive to Nantes and —"

"To Nantes! But if they've driven to Nantes and —"

"Be calm, please. It means only that instead of taking you back in my car, I shall take you in the cart. It is very comfortable. Then when I have left you, I shall return it to its stable. Come."

She saw no point in arguing. She saw no point in saying anything, except to herself for having been unwise enough to involve herself in a situation that left her stranded in a field ringed by poplars and with no transportation except a cart that, she realized as she clambered into it, when not being used to convey artists, was used for carting dung.

"You are comfortable?" Pierre asked, as they left the rutted approach and the cart regained its equilibrium on the main road.

"No, I'm not. But thanks for asking."

"It was a mistake to bring you, this is clear. You did not listen to the music, you did not study the painting. I should not have brought you."

"Bringing me was one thing. Handing over your car —"

"Please consider. If they missed the train, if they did not get to Paris in time, what would happen? For you and me, it is only a question of a little inconvenience. For them, it is a serious, a very serious thing. They have to earn a living. They are to appear punctually at the rehearsal tomorrow."

"Today."

"Today. Korsmann is conducting; he is magnificent, almost as good as my father, but everybody knows his temper; if the musicians are not in their places, waiting for him, then he is like a devil. He —"

"Look" — the horse had slithered on a wet patch of road, throwing Kerry forward — "couldn't you persuade this animal to stop galloping?"

"He is anxious to get home."

How anxious, they presently discovered. At a junction of the road, Pierre indicated his desire to go to the left. The horse manifested as strong a wish to turn right. Checked in this hope, it stood stock still. Wheedling and threats had no effect. Even the application of the whip, a stringlike object resembling a fly whisk, failed to move the animal.

"You hold the reins. I will lead him a little way," Pierre said.

He led the horse a few hundred yards. It waited until he got into the cart and then made a swift turn and broke into a gallop, hurling Pierre onto Kerry's lap. Righting himself, he clutched the reins and pulled them, without effect. Through the softly lit night they raced, leaving behind them the glow in the sky that was the reflection of the lights of Gaston-le-Grand.

"He will not stop," Pierre said unnecessarily. "I do not in a way blame him."

They sped past the hostel, now in total darkness. Half a mile beyond it, the horse checked with an abruptness that nearly threw them out of the cart and then turned at a slower but still purposeful gait onto a narrow country lane. Ahead they could see the outlines of farm buildings. The horse walked quietly through a wide gateway and came to a halt outside the stables.

"He's home," Kerry said calmly. "How about us?"

"It is no use trying to make him go again."

"No use at all," she agreed.

They unharnessed the animal and led him into the stable and made him comfortable. No light sprang up in the farmhouse, nobody appeared. Exploring the sheds, they found a plow, a tractor, a bicycle with one wheel missing and a child's carriage, but nothing they could have borrowed to take them back to the town.

"We must walk," Pierre announced at last.

She glanced at her shoes. They were not the kind she would have chosen for a tramp along country lanes, but at least they were low-heeled, and they were comfortable.

"I am to blame," Pierre said as they left the farm behind, "for not driving my car myself to the station. There was time, only just time, but still time enough for them to catch the train; but when other people drive it, they do not understand the engine and sometimes it is not reliable. So I think they broke down. I should have gone with them, but I wanted to see the work that Claud and Georges were doing."

She said nothing. They were plodding along damp paths beside little streams, following shortcuts that Pierre remembered from his boyhood. They went sometimes abreast, sometimes one behind the other. Having got into his stride in more senses than one, Pierre talked, telling her the history of the hostel and the series of hopeful aspirants to fame who had worked there, the Leonies and the Bernards and the Clauds, poor, dedicated, eager, struggling, undaunted by early lack of success. He spoke of his father's visits in the early days — but not lately, he explained, because although all was over between Madame Daumier and himself, his wife had pointed out that it was foolish to come back and be so near her, so near the house in which he had so regrettably installed her. While he talked, Kerry did mental arithmetic, filling in details on the chart of the past that she was attempting to make for herself and for Dale. Eighteen years ago, Professor Thorwaldsen. Fifteen years ago, Lord Hazing. Where did the Drummond episode fit? Albert Leclair was the easiest to place. They had come here when Pierre was fifteen or a little more and they had stayed, she was now learning, until Albert had returned to Paris to give what help he could to his son on the threshold of his career. Four years. Albert had gone, Madeleine had remained in the house . . .

"This way. It is shorter," Pierre said.

They had been walking toward the town; now they had turned onto a path that led directly to the sea.

"We shall come out at last behind the Maison du Bois," Pierre told her. "Then we shall climb the hill."

When they clambered up the slope and reached the top, she stopped for the first time since leaving the farm — and it was not from fatigue.

"Oh, look!" she exclaimed, and her tone was eloquent.

They were not standing at any great height, but at their feet lay three separate and distinct aspects of Gaston-le-Grand. Immediately below was the secluded semicircle of beach now familiar to her, with the four large houses and the winking lights of the harbour. To the right she could see the full extent of the larger beach, with its now-shuttered wooden shacks and its still-lit neon signs. To the left, thick pinewoods dropped almost to sea level, becoming lost in the vague, shadowy shapes of the rocks.

"When I was a little boy," Pierre said dreamily, "I used to like to go and play on that other beach. My mother did not like me to go, because the girls were very bold. There was a bandstand once; on special days — something municipal, or perhaps saints' feasts — a band would play. It was not a good band, simply volunteers from among the shopkeepers, but I got to know some of the musicians, and I used to look for them on the beach. Sometimes I would go home with them and they would let me play their instruments. There was a drawing master among them, and he asked to see some of my work and said he could not teach me anything."

There was a backless bench near them. Kerry sat on it and made room for him beside her.

"When did you first decide between music and painting?" she asked him.

"I always knew what I would do. But for my father's sake, I tried to change, because he wanted me to follow him. I think he regrets the years he spent with your mother, because he will never be sure, quite sure, whether he could have influenced me to give up painting. I am sure that he could not, but in his mind there will always be a doubt. But he is happy because I will be as famous as he was. My mother is happy because I sell my pictures well. She does not believe that a man should pursue his art too long if it does not make a living for him. She is wrong, but it doesn't matter. The only thing she does not understand is why I prefer to live in my own apartment. I left my parents' house when I was twenty, and my mother was angry, because to spend money on two establishments seemed to her wasteful. But she got used to it, and I am not far away and she can ask me to go and see her when she needs me — as she needed me when she found that your mother had written to my father."

"Why should she worry, after all these years?"

"She would worry more if she could see your mother. I have never met a woman of her age who seems so young. Why did you stay here with her? You told me that you came with a message, not knowing who she was. When you knew, why did you stay? Was it because you were glad to find your mother at last, or was it simply to learn more about her? Or was it — this I think is the most likely — to find out everything about your father?"

"All three, I suppose."

"Where is your father now?"

"I've no idea."

"You've — you've . . ." His voice died away in astonishment. "How can you have no idea? Your aunts, those aunts who brought you up, they of course must know. They didn't tell you?"

"They didn't know where he was or who he was. I don't know where he is or who he is."

"But this is fantastic! You didn't ask your mother these things?"

"Yes."

"She refused to answer?"

"She's writing to ask his permission."

"*Permission? Permission?* Permission to tell his children —"

"Well, use your head. If he's happily married and —"

"You are his children. If he is a normal man, he will want to see you and your sister. If he learns that you are here with your mother, he will even come here. Even if he comes only from curiosity, he will wish to see you. But perhaps he is not a normal man. I am a normal man, and if I had children, I would not consent to let them go away from me so that I did not know where they were."

"You might, in certain circumstances."

"In no certain circumstances whatever. If I quarrelled with my wife, that is one thing. This can happen. If we had young children when we quarrelled, and she wanted to go away from me, I would not prevent her; sometimes I think it will not be easy for a wife to live with me. If she went away, she would have to take the children if they were very young, to look after them. But to take them forever, to take them away from me, whose flesh they are, whose as you could say creation, even immortality, this I would never permit. Never. A man who would do this is not, I think, a good man. And a woman who allows her children to go out of her care, out of her life — this I understand even less. Did you ask your mother what excuse she could give for this?"

"No. But if you're following men round the world, how can you drag young children with you? That's why she handed us over to the aunts."

"Drag? Following? She used these words to you?"

"No. But if she had done, I'd have been less upset than you seem to be."

"If that is so, we — you and I — do not speak the same language in any sense of this term. You could leave your children, as she did?"

"No, I couldn't. But —"

"Do not continue with *but*. I am happy to be reassured."

"Instead of criticizing my mother, why don't you take a look at your own?" Kerry suggested. "Maybe she didn't abandon you, but why didn't she look after you properly? Why didn't she feed you? You're nothing but a bag of bones."

"My mother fed me well. I eat, I ate everything. Simply, I don't get fat. I am not the fat kind of man. I do not like fat men."

"Who said anything about fat? Don't your girlfriends complain?"

"Complain? Girlfriends?"

"If you embraced a woman, which I admit sounds a pretty unlikely possibility from what I know of you, she'd think she'd been trapped in a steel cage."

"You are not polite. I eat bread, potatoes. I eat pies. I eat and drink everything known to make weight, but it does not make weight for me."

"Then you must be burning it up too fast. Why don't you relax?"

"What do you mean by relax?"

"Cut out some of these music sessions. They make you overexcited and —"

"You mean that I must only paint? You are not serious, I think. I have noticed that you make things into a joke. Music, for me, comes second only to painting."

"Where does fun come?"

"Fun? If you mean to be happy, I am happy all the time. My days are full, with painting, with concerts, with artists, with composers. If you are asking me how I amuse myself, that is how, that is when. All the time, I am doing what I love to do. Is this fun?"

"I suppose so."

"But you, you like to dance, to go to parties to drink and to talk? Perhaps this is your kind of fun?"

"No."

"Then?"

"Well, I suppose you'd say I went in for sport."

"Sport?"

"I swim, as you saw. I ice skate. I ride and I play tennis. As I said, sport."

"But this is only for exercise of the body. There is also the mind, and the spirit. Music? No, I saw this evening that you did not understand what they were playing. Painting? Perhaps instead of teaching you French, I should —"

"There's no time to fill in gaps. Next week I'll

be back in London and you'll be back in Paris."

"Are you going so soon?"

"I shouldn't be here at all. If I hadn't met my mother, I would have been touring the châteaux country in a beautiful car."

"I can show you the châteaux, but not in a beautiful car. Who would have driven this beautiful car? A man?"

"Yes."

"A fat man, of the kind you like? When you did not go, what did you say to him? Did you say: I have met my mother after so long, I cannot go with you?"

"I sent a telegram saying the trip was off."

"You did not tell him why?"

"In a telegram? Of course not. If he asks me when I see him again — if I see him again — I'll tell him."

She got to her feet, stretched, yawned and saw him rising, and noted with some relief that it was with reluctance. There was something disturbing in the thought that a man had walked with her in the moonlight, sat with her in the moonlight and had talked only of her mother and his mother.

"You begin to talk," he complained, "and then you rush away, like from the beach this afternoon."

"Yesterday afternoon. You don't have to come down to the house with me; I can get there safely by myself."

"I shall go with you. It will remind me of the

times when I was a boy and came this way."

"At dawn?"

"Once, yes, at dawn. I went to bed at the normal hour, and then I got up again, climbed from my bed and went into the town to meet a girl."

"At fifteen!"

"Fourteen. It was the circus."

"Ah. She wore a tutu and rode a big, white horse?"

"No. She took money at the entrance of the tent. She said I could earn money by playing the violin for the clown who had a violin but who could not play. He pretended to play only. So on this night that I am telling you about, I played from behind the curtains and nobody knew that it was not the clown."

"Did you play until dawn?"

"No. After the performance, I stayed with them. It was exciting for a young boy. They were artists, too, and professional. This, all my life, I have recognized — the difference between those who work by routine and those who are driven by their art. There are two worlds, and I have only lived in one."

They walked down the steep slope, his hand on her arm to prevent her from slipping. Behind them, Gaston-le-Grand still slept. The four houses were dark and silent. Only the porch of the Maison du Bois glowed, and the harbour lights were reflected in the black water.

"Goodbye," he said at the wicker gate. "I am

sorry. I do not think that you enjoyed yourself tonight."

"Last night. I wouldn't have missed it for anything. Goodbye."

"Shall I see you tomorrow, today?"

"Yes. On the beach."

He watched her until she reached the door. She went up to her room and undressed and went to bed, thinking with some surprise that her assurance to him had been the truth: she would not have liked to miss anything of the past few hours. She was not clear what, if anything, had come out of the experience, but it had left her with a curious sense of peace. Perhaps it came from the fact that this man, far from handsome, untidy, vain, disorganized and dedicated, was like nobody she had met before. There had been a kind of companionship on the walk from the farmhouse that had been free from any of the problems that usually arose between herself and the men she met.

It was restful, she decided, settling down to sleep, to be with a man who didn't create tensions. All the same, you could say that it was rather a waste of a lovely night and a lovely moon.

Chapter Eight

It was past ten o'clock when Kerry opened her eyes, and the fact that she had slept so late marked yet another change from her working life and the routine past; she could not remember ever over-sleeping. She got out of bed, opened the shutters wide and stood looking out at the sunlit scene. The fishing boats were coming into harbour. The door of the little hut on the quay stood open, and around it a knot of people were standing idly, the most idle of all the official with the peaked cap whose functions she had not yet discovered but who was there, she thought, to examine yachts-men's papers and to keep a lookout for smugglers.

A light knock on the door made her turn. Her mother spoke from the threshold.

"I heard you open your window. Good morning, Kerry."

She was already dressed, sleeveless and cool and uncrushable. She made way for Clothilde and the breakfast tray; then she sat on the stool in front of the dressing table. Kerry sat on the bed and unfolded her napkin.

"Did you hear me come in?" she asked.

"No."

"Pierre brought me back. We walked."

"Walked?"

"He lent his car to some students and we assumed they'd missed the train and driven on to Nantes."

"You walked all the way from the hostel?"

"From the farm. We started off in a cart, but the horse wouldn't cooperate."

She paused; there was no comment from her mother. It was difficult, she thought, to know whether that stillness meant that she was listening with rapt attention or merely thinking of other matters. She could understand a man returning at the end of the day to this soft, accommodating cushion into which he could sink while he unburdened his mind of problems; they would clarify themselves as he put them into words, and all the while he could refresh his eyes with her beauty. It was easy to believe that in this tranquillity, a man might accomplish his best work.

There must surely, she mused, be some inquiry about the Professor's departure, apart from the few words over the telephone the previous evening. She waited expectantly, but felt no undue surprise when her mother's next words proved that the Professor had been relegated to the past from which he had so inconveniently emerged.

"When you were out yesterday, Kerry, something happened."

Kerry smiled inwardly. This was going to be no surprise.

"Not long after you drove away, there was a

visitor. Clothilde went to the door. I happened to be going downstairs, and I met her coming up with the card, and there was no way of pretending that I was out, because he was there in the hall, and he looked up and saw me."

"He?"

"The fourth man I wrote to. Benjamin Drummond. I couldn't believe — Do you know, Kerry, that you actually spoke to him, I mean to him and his wife, on the beach?"

"The Americans?"

"Yes. That's their yacht in the harbour — the big one. No, not theirs; he hired it to come here. His wife was with him, and his children, but he came in answer to my letter. He told his wife he was going to walk round the town, and he came to see me, and — you can imagine what a shock it was!"

"Yes." Kerry spread honey on her toast. "Yes, I can."

"I came down and we went into the drawing room and talked. It was hard to think that it was so long ago. Years and years."

"How many years exactly?"

Madame Daumier hesitated. She might be slow at counting, or she might be anxious not to give too much away, Kerry thought.

"Twelve years. I was thirty-three when I left him. We'd had three very happy years together, but it just proved, when he came yesterday, that you can never go back to the past, because I didn't feel the same about him at all. In fact, I found myself thinking that he was not the type of man I would have said I liked. It just shows you. But he's still very good-looking."

Kerry was doing some more arithmetic. So Benjamin Drummond followed Lord Hazing. And Christian Thorwaldsen preceded Lord Hazing and so, of course, did her father. But her mother hadn't stayed with her father into her late twenties, so there was still a piece or two missing. It occurred to her that if she had not been so grieved over the Professor's plight, she might have been able to find out something about the past that concerned her far more vitally than it had concerned him. But it was too late; he had gone, and the opportunity with him.

"Did you tell Mr. Drummond you'd got the money for the house?" she asked.

"Oh Kerry, how could I? When he'd come all this way in a specially hired yacht, how could I tell him that he'd come for nothing?"

Kerry poured herself out more coffee and drank it thoughtfully. There were some things, she felt, that it was going to be difficult, if not impossible, to convey to Dale. Dale would expect facts, but what were the facts about their mother? Was she tenderhearted, or hard as stone? Was she mercenary, or driven only by the longing to buy this house? Was she devious, or was she stupid? It would be easy for a stupid woman to deceive the Professor. But the smooth, worldly, experienced Benjamin Drummond? The keen-eyed, brilliant, dynamic Lord Hazing?

She could not believe it.

"The only man I ever found it hard to forget," her mother said pensively, "was your father. I think he was the only man I ever really loved. The proof is —"

She stopped abruptly. Whatever the proof was, Kerry realized she was not going to be allowed to test it. After a pause during which Madame Daumier apparently recovered from the shock of having almost given something away, she went on speaking.

"The others . . . I thought at the time that I was in love, but looking back, I know that all I was looking for was security. A home."

They would have been surprised, those others, Kerry thought, to know that she regarded them not as virile lovers, but as roofs and gables.

"I think that without meaning to," her mother summed up, "I often raised false hopes."

"How long did Mr. Drummond stay?"

"He had tea here. He was here for about three hours but it didn't seem so long. He's going back to St. Malo tomorrow."

"So soon?"

"Yes. He knows that you're my daughter."

"You told him?"

"On the beach, you said that you were staying at the Maison du Bois with your mother. So you told him."

"Did you mind his knowing?"

"No. He knew that I had two children. I said that you had come here on business — that's true, isn't it? — and that we'd met and recognized one another."

"Did you mention Pierre Leclair?"

"No."

"Did you tell him you'd written to anybody else about the house?"

"No."

They were gentle, softly spoken negatives, but Kerry sensed something firm behind them. There was no reason to mention Pierre Leclair to Benjamin Drummond unless . . . But that would be too fantastic. And yet, would it? The past was being turned into the present, and three of the men recalled by her mother's letters were certainly linked; was it too much to suppose that Benjamin Drummond would know the name Leclair?

Her mother had risen. The subject appeared to be closed.

"I'm going down to the beach when I'm dressed. Why don't you come with me?" she asked.

Madame Daumier shook her head.

"I'm sorry. I can't. Some people have arrived at the house —"

"Oh, the General?"

Madame Daumier's hand seemed to freeze on its way to the door handle. Turning, she gave Kerry the long, blank, now-familiar blue stare.

"Did you say — You *know* him?"

"No. But Pierre and I ran into a sister of his at

the station, so I knew they were the tenants of Villa Azul."

"His sister?"

"So she told us."

"I didn't know his sister was going to stay with him."

"Neither did he. A nice little surprise, she called it. Have you ever met her?"

Madame Daumier shuddered.

"Years ago. Many, many years ago. She was a dreadful woman."

"She still is."

"So *that*," Madame Daumier said, "is why he didn't come to see me last night. Monsieur Courbet wanted me to go out to lunch with him today, and I refused because I was sure the General would have some plan. But if his sister is with him, I shall keep out of her way."

"Would she really come without being invited?"

"If she waited for invitations, would she ever go anywhere?"

"I suppose not. She must be hoping to stay for the season; she was fetching a huge trunk."

"Poor, poor Gerald. One reason for coming out here every year was to get away from her." Madame Daumier sighed. "I shall tell Monsieur Courbet that I'm free for lunch after all. Do you mind lunching alone, Kerry?"

"Not in the least. But if you're going to be out, could I have a packed lunch to take to the beach?"

"Of course. I'll tell Clothilde."

"Would you ask her to pack enough for two? With lots of fattening things."

"Two?"

"I'm giving Pierre Leclair swimming lessons. He's so thin that just looking at him makes me feel starved. May I borrow your beach robe again?"

"Of course."

She did not offer to bring it, and Kerry did not expect her to. One of the few things she had learned about her mother was that if a bell was within reach, she would press it, and that would be all.

She walked across the landing, some time later, in her bathing suit. Coming out of her mother's room with the beach robe, she glanced out the window and saw Monsieur Courbet's car. The chauffeur was standing beside it; Monsieur Courbet was handing her mother in. It was difficult to decide from his back view whether he was looking fatherly, or not. He had certainly leaped with alacrity into the breach caused by Miss Arran-Duff.

She took the picnic basket and went down to the beach. Pierre was waiting for her at the foot of the steps, gaunt in his maroon trunks and no longer bleached, but blistered.

"I couldn't sleep," he complained. "See how burned I am."

"Why couldn't you have used some of my suntan lotion? Now you'll peel."

"Already I am peeling — look. Why are you so late?"

"I overslept. I've brought our picnic lunch."

"Our?"

"I've decided to fatten you up. That's why the basket's so heavy."

He spread her towel and sat down beside her.

"Which do we do first?" she asked him. "French or swimming?"

"We shall swim," he said unhesitatingly, "and then we shall speak French, and when we become dry we can swim again. In this way we shall —"

"— get two swimming lessons for one French lesson. Look." She nodded toward the group trudging along the sand toward them. "The Drummonds."

"Who?"

When they came up, Mrs. Drummond greeted Kerry with obvious pleasure.

"It's good to see you," she said, dropping her burdens in a heap on the sand and sitting beside her. "I was afraid that maybe you wouldn't come, and I'd be stuck here alone with the kids. Priss! Come here and put on your arm bands. Ben's coming down later, he says, but he doesn't always do what he says."

Kerry performed brief introductions, and the children joined them. Jumbo stared in astonishment at Pierre.

"Gee, you're kinda skinny, aren't you?" he exclaimed.

"That is what Miss Cromer is always saying."

"Hey, you talk like a Frenchie," Jumbo said.

"That is what I am. And you are an Americano. Do you speak French?"

"Sort of. I'd talk it better, but my mother keeps going back to America, so I keep forgetting it."

"I will teach you. I am teaching Miss Cromer."

"What's your other name?" Jumbo asked irritably, turning to Kerry. "I don't go for that Miss stuff."

"Now, Jumbo, that's rude," his mother told him. "Go and swim, if you're going to swim."

"Well, I'm not," he said. "I'm going to finish my drawing. Why couldn't I stay on the yacht and finish it?"

"Because your father wanted to be quiet."

"What's noisy about drawing?" Jumbo demanded. He dropped peevishly onto the sand and opened a large and very dirty drawing book. "I suppose he thought my pencil would squeak, or somepin. I bet he's making a noise now, popping corks."

"Jumbo," his mother said, scandalized, "don't you dare —"

"Aw, lemme draw, will ya?" Jumbo yelled. "Yap, yap and —" He stopped and looked at Pierre. "What?"

"I said," Pierre repeated, "that the tail is wrong."

He was looking at the drawing on the page that Jumbo had opened. He held out a hand.

"Give me your pencil."

Surprised, Jumbo handed it to him and leaned over to watch Pierre's hand moving swiftly over the half-finished sketch of a squirrel. The tail grew bushy and thick and at last became an appendage so lifelike that Jumbo's hand moved toward it as though to stroke it.

"Gee!" he breathed in awe. "Gee, I wish I could do that!"

"You can," Pierre said. "You can draw. You can draw well."

Jumbo stared at him, his manner bristling.

"You kidding?" he inquired in a high, furious tone. "You are, aren't you? You're just saying that. You don't mean it."

"If I didn't mean it, I would not dream of saying it," Pierre assured him with patent sincerity. "I myself am an artist; I would not tell you what was not true about your work. Show me the other things."

"I haven't got any other things here. Only on the yacht."

"Do you paint, too?"

"Yeah, sure. I can paint anything," Jumbo asserted with an air that Kerry thought exactly like Pierre's when he made similar claims. "I paint. I paint all the time. Ask my mother."

"He paints all right," Mrs. Drummond corroborated. "You should see his grandmother's house. He's painted all over it."

"Not" — Pierre gazed at Jumbo — "not on the *walls?*" he asked slowly.

Jumbo, about to return a defiant answer,

paused. There was something in the tone that puzzled him.

"Sure, on the walls," he said. "If you want to paint real big, where else can you get to do it?"

"Murals, so young!" breathed Pierre. "I, too," he told Jumbo, "I painted murals when I was a small boy."

"Murals?"

"*Mur,* a wall. Mural. In the yacht in which you have come from St. Malo, there is a mural I painted in the saloon. It was what is called a commission; that means that they ask you to do it, and pay you a lot of money. Haven't you seen my work in the saloon of the yacht?"

"The — *you* did that?"

"Yes. You like it?"

"Sure. But nobody else does. My mother says she doesn't know what it is."

"Jumbo, I didn't *say* that," Mrs. Drummond said in confusion. "I just —"

"You just said it was enough to put people off their food, that's what you said. You didn't even know what it was!" Jumbo shouted.

"And you?" Pierre asked him. "You knew what it was?"

"Yeah. It's something you're looking at in the water. That's right, isn't it?"

"A reflection, yes."

"My mother thought it was upside down."

"And she was right. And that is one mural which nobody will ever be able to take away, unless the ship goes down to the bottom of the sea.

Will your grandmother leave your paintings on the walls?"

"She promised. She's pretty old, but she says when she dies, she'll tell my father and mother not to touch 'em."

"Good. She is a farseeing person," Pierre said. "And now it is time for my swimming lesson."

The lesson would have been more successful if Jumbo had not elected to supervise it. Like his brother, he swam easily and well, though neither he nor Pete made any attempt to assist their sister Priss, who, arm bands inflated, ran screaming toward the water and at the approach of even the smallest wave, turned and ran screaming back to the shore. Now, as Kerry coached the floundering Pierre, Jumbo trod water close by, his small face puckered in anxiety, his salt-reddened eyes following every movement of his new hero. When, blue and shivering, Pierre stood at last on the beach, it was Jumbo who begged him to go for a run.

"Aw, come on," he urged. "You'll catch a cold. You'll get pneumonia. You've got to run fast. Come on, I'll take you."

They streaked away, the thin long figure and the thin small figure, and Kerry walked slowly back to the tent. Mrs. Drummond, sitting propped against a rubber backrest, looked at her anxiously.

"Is Pierre offended?" she asked

"Heavens, no! He didn't mind."

"That's Jumbo all over; he opens his mouth,

and nobody knows what's going to come out. And that mural — well, wait till you see it, that's all. Even Ben couldn't take it, and he likes to think he's artistic. He even goes to art sales. Was there an art sale in Gaston-le-Grand yesterday afternoon?"

"I don't know."

"Well, that's where he said he went, to look at it. I told you, didn't I, that he didn't bring us all down here in such a hurry just to breathe sea air? At times like this, I miss my mother-in-law. The way comedians go on, you'd think all mothers-in-law were terrible, but Ben's mother and I always get along, and what she doesn't know about men as a whole, and about Ben in particular, would fit on that squirrel's tail. I knew Ben had come here on some kind of sexy business, finished or unfinished, but his mother would've known which. I could only guess, when he got back yesterday."

"And did you guess finished, or unfinished?" Kerry smiled.

"Well —" Mrs. Drummond hesitated. "For one thing, we're leaving here tomorrow, he says. So that sounds finished, doesn't it?"

"Yes."

"On the other hand, he came back looking — what's the word? Well, it's the way he looks when he brings off a business deal and knows he's come out on the right end of it. *That* sort of look."

"Don't you ever ask him any questions?"

"No. I don't have to. What I mean is that mostly he tells me when it's all over, but asking questions wouldn't be any good, because you wouldn't get anything out of him that he didn't want you to know. He might tell me, one day, what we came down here for, but then again, he mightn't."

"Wouldn't he have come by himself, if it was the sort of business you've got in mind?"

"That he'd got in mind, you mean. No. He couldn't have come by himself because we were all packed up and ready to ride. Whoever and whatever it was, he was stuck with us. So we all came along, and it hasn't been too bad and I'm not grumbling or beefing or kicking, but what I feel is that we're not getting any younger, Ben and I, and someday he'll have to start thinking of his blood pressure and lay off these little trips on the side." She threw a glance at Kerry. "Maybe you think it's funny, a total stranger like me showing you my husband's graph, but I suppose people have done it before. You're a girl who gives people a sort of feeling you're not a blabbermouth. And I don't find many people to talk to, in Paris. You'd think with a population like it's got, I'd be able to pick out somebody to let my wig down with, but what with getting the children to school, and shopping in French, and putting out drinks for Ben's business buddies, I don't seem to get time to make any real friends. But Ben feels the way I do about you, because last night, when we got talking, he said you'd

200

stuck in his mind, which meant that he thought you were pretty attractive. He wondered why you hadn't gotten married, and I said I thought it wouldn't be long, because you can always tell when a girl's hooked. She —"

She paused. Kerry, who had been lying back, half-listening, half-dreaming, had sat up with a jerk and was staring at her.

"*What* did you say?" she asked in astonishment

"About you? Only that it stuck out a mile."

"*What* stuck out a mile?"

"That look."

"What look?"

"You get it every time you look at that Frenchman. You —"

"*Pierre?*"

"Sure. Pierre. Every time you look at him, there it is — that look. You can't mistake it. If you don't know you're hooked, and if you want to know what you look like when you look at him, then watch Jumbo. He's hooked, too. His eyes look just like yours when he turns 'em on Pierre."

"If you mean I worry a bit about him because he's too thin —"

"Yes, that's what I mean. Hooked. It starts that way. If you really don't know yet, maybe I should have let it creep up on you — but if there's one trap that's more dangerous than any other in this game, it's that protective feeling. 'You bring out, not the gypsy in me, but the mother in me.' That feeling. It's how you feel when you can't bear cats, but you hear a mew and there in the yard there's a bedraggled kitten with its ribs showing, and you still don't like cats, but that kitten's on a blanket in the kitchen, lapping cream. See what I mean?"

Kerry had no comment to make. Denial would be childish, and though she could have argued and in the end proved that in this case rescue operations would proceed no further than the yard, there was something about Mrs. Drummond's flat, unemphatic, sensible and experienced manner that forced her to give serious consideration to what she had said.

She came out of a daze to realize that Pierre had assembled all the children on the beach and had lined them up. Holding a shovel by the digging end, he was about to conduct a choir.

"Please to stand still. Two will stand here, so. Now — Ah, already you know what I am going to do! Now we have an international choir. Here is what we shall do. First, the two here shall sing this note: Ahhhhh. Up, up — yes, that is true, that is beautiful. Now the next group. You will please to sing this: Looooooo. Good, good, very good. Now you, please. Laaaaaaaa. Perfect. Now the last: Leeeeeeeee. Now we are ready. *Écoute, mes enfants.* Please to sing your own notes. No, no, do not listen at all to what anybody else is singing. Close your ears and sing only your own note. Now. Perfect. *Magnifique.* Now please to watch my hands. When I point to you, you shall sing your note. When not, not. Now the others at the end, they will sing this melody —"

When he raised his shovel to command silence, he got it. And then, for all to hear, came a four-part rendering of the familiar "Frère Jacques." The children, suddenly aware of the harmony, sang in amazement and pride, but their eyes did not leave the conductor. Parents, guardians and friends drew near, formed a ring and listened in wonder.

"Well!" Mrs. Drummond addressed Kerry in a tone of awe. "That's the first time I've ever seen any of my children doing what they were told. D'you think he'd care to adopt Jumbo?" she ended hopefully.

There were indications, when the choir dispersed, that Jumbo had done the adopting. His eyes followed Pierre with an expression that Kerry was relieved to see held nothing maternal whatsoever, but that promised a fight to anybody rash enough to comment on his behaviour.

Mr. Drummond, who had arrived in time to hear the last few bars, joined them and expressed himself delighted to find Pierre on friendly terms with his family.

"How about lunch on board?" he suggested. "After that grand performance, we'd be proud to have you. We'll be able to have some music on board, because there's a piano in the saloon. I think it's a piano. It looks like a piano, but nobody's ever opened it to find out. Miss Cromer, Kerry, will you come?"

She pointed to the picnic basket.

"Oh, come on!" he protested. "We can give you something better than sandwiches. We can give you a long, cool drink, too, and I hope you don't need it as much as I do. I don't go for this sand-between-the-toes stuff. Let's all get onto that yacht and sit on something that doesn't stick to your skin."

Kerry glanced at Pierre.

"If Pierre —" She stopped. If she refused to go, Mrs. Drummond would regard the refusal as a sign that she wanted to stay in the yard and share the cream. "Thank you. We'd love to come," she said.

They walked toward the harbour, negotiated the rocks and the pools, clambered onto the quay and divided themselves into two groups and two dinghies: the one belonging to the yacht, and the one hired from the official in the hut. Mr. Drummond, in the first party with Pierre, was waiting to assist Kerry and his wife aboard.

"Pierre's just been telling me he's been on this boat before," he told his wife. "He knows the owner."

"I know him very well," Pierre said. "I always tell him that he charges too much for these charters. No French person would pay so much."

"Well, she's comfortable," Mr. Drummond said, "and there's plenty of deck space, and so many stewards that you fall over them whenever you try to move. And there's the piano I told you about, and murals, too, can you beat that? Murals."

"Yeah," said Jumbo. "He —"

"Quiet, Jumbo," his father admonished. "I'm talking."

"O.K. Talk," Jumbo said grimly. "Just talk."

"Yes, murals," resumed Mr. Drummond. "I couldn't have them moved, because murals don't move."

"Unfortunately, sometimes they do," Pierre said gloomily.

"I wish these would. They're terrible, really terrible," Mr. Drummond said, "and —"

"And he did them!" Jumbo shouted furiously. "He did them. He painted them. Pierre did. Ask him. I *told* you they were good, didn't I? I told you, but you didn't listen."

"Do you expect," Pierre asked him, "that everyone should like the same pictures?"

"No, but —"

"If you painted the reflections in the water near this boat — come and look at them. See them? They are never still; however calm the water may be, you will see a quiver, a slight movement of what is reflected. You and I are looking now at the same scene, but if we painted it now, sitting here together, your canvas and mine would look quite different, because my eyes are my eyes, and your eyes are your eyes. Come inside with me and we shall look at the mural and you will tell me exactly why I painted it in that way."

Jumbo led him toward the saloon; the other two children followed on their heels, and Mrs. Drummond brought up the rear. Mr. Drummond and Kerry were left on the deck, comfortable on long, cushioned wicker chairs. On the neighbouring boat, the crew worked busily, coiling ropes and polishing brass; it seemed to Kerry hard labour to choose on such a warm afternoon. Gulls swooped down to the water in search of tidbits and, disappointed, soared skyward again. A youth paddled by in an inflated canoe.

Mr. Drummond leaned over to spear an olive from the dish on the table between them and sat twisting it contemplatively. Kerry knew that he was preparing to introduce the subject that was uppermost in both their minds. He spoke at last with his eyes still on the olive.

"Well, Kerry?" His tone was quiet. "So now you know why I came to Gaston-le-Grand." He raised his eyes to meet hers. "Did you talk to your mother this morning?"

"Yes. She told me you'd been to see her."

"When I spoke to you on the beach yesterday," he said slowly, "who would have dreamed . . . How much did she tell you?"

"Just the fact that you'd gone to the house. How much did she tell you?"

"You came here on business, and recognized one another. And that was almost all. She was never a talker."

"I know that she wrote to you and asked for

money. But she didn't expect you to reply in person."

"My God!" he said in a tone of wonder. "It takes a woman to do a thing like that. A letter, after all these years, asking for, well, a sizable sum of money, and expecting to get it in an envelope by return of post, with nothing dredged up from the dead past."

"Did you read it as an invitation?"

He turned his head to study her.

"An invitation? No. No, not exactly that."

"Did it sound like a wish to —"

"— see me again? Start things all over again? No. I guess it was just a chance to see her, and I took it."

"Are you sorry?"

"I'm not disappointed, if that's what you mean. I wanted to see her again. I wanted to find out what she'd got that shook me so hard when I was, I thought, past the age to lose my head. I was no younger, and I wouldn't have said, when I first saw her, that she'd be the kind of woman I'd go overboard for. Even now, I can't explain it. But no, I wasn't disappointed. I thought I'd been lucky to hold her for as long as I did. She hasn't changed much, but I guess that this time, I looked at her differently. And I realized that I didn't want to have it all over again."

"Then you *are* sorry you came."

"Hell, no." He paused and then spoke thoughtfully. "It brought back a lot of memories, all pretty nice ones. It was fun, Kerry. God, it was fun. I didn't seem to need, with her, any of the things I'd needed before or have needed since. I'm said to be a good man at a party; in American terms, that means I'm a social character, that I get around and meet people, mix in, keep up with the boys. I guess that about sums me up, and I enjoy being what I am. But with her, for those three years, it was different. I wanted to stay home, if you can call hotels home. I never wanted to get into a crowd. If I went out, I wanted to go out with her, and just her and nobody else. Dinner somewhere, just the two of us. Walks. Drives. Church, too. I'm a Catholic and she used to come to mass with me. She was a woman who gave you the feeling that she was contented all the time. You didn't have to ask her, it just seemed to be there, inside her. When you were with her, you felt a sort of — a sort of serenity. Peace. You didn't worry about anything. You relaxed. You felt that everything was going along all right. She never argued, she never quarrelled, she never raised her voice. How many women have you met who have her quiet, soft, musical voice? If I'm making her sound dull, I'm telling it badly. Those were hard years from the business angle; sometimes I think that it was because she was what she was, restful, like some kind of tranquilizer, that I managed to pull the firm out of its troubles. You know, Kerry, when I look back on that interlude — because that's all it turned out to be, an interlude; she never agreed to marry me — when I look back, I don't seem to see myself clearly. I look like some other guy, a guy something like me, but with the froth skimmed off. A happy guy. I'm happy now, I guess, but in a different way. I love my wife and my kids, my wife all the time and my kids some of the time, but I have to work at it. During those three years with your mother, it was just there." He paused. "Yesterday, it wasn't there anymore, and that's kind of thrown me out of my stride, because no man likes to realize that what he was in love with was his own reflection." He shot her a worried glance. "Maybe I shouldn't have said that. Are you angry?"

"No. Grateful. You've cleared up something for me. Will you clear up something else?"

"What is it?"

"Do you know what Pierre's name is? His surname, I mean."

"Pierre? This Pierre, the mural Pierre? No, I don't. Should I?"

"He's Pierre Leclair. His father was, is, a famous conductor."

He did not speak for so long that she began to wonder if he had heard. Then he spoke in a soft, astounded tone.

"Well, I'll be damned." He twisted around to stare at her. "*That* Leclair?"

"Yes."

"Does your mother know he's here?"

"Yes."

"She didn't say one damn, one goddamn word about him to me."

209

"I wouldn't have mentioned him either, if I hadn't been curious to fill in some gaps. Pierre came here because my mother wrote to his father, for money. His father wanted to come — for the same reasons, I suppose, as the ones you've just given me — but Pierre came instead."

"I'll fill in one gap for you. I filled the gap between a guy called Hazing — Lord Hazing — and the conductor, Leclair."

"Thank you. One of the other things my mother didn't tell you was that I work for Lord Hazing."

It was interesting, she thought, to have silenced for the second time in the course of a brief conversation a man as articulate as Benjamin Drummond. He was sitting staring at her, his jaw dropped. At last he closed his mouth, shook his head to clear it, and sat up straighter in his chair.

"Say that again," he requested. "Maybe I didn't get it right. I get buzzes in the ear sometimes. Now: what was that you said?"

"I work for Lord Hazing. He sent me here. Like you and Albert Leclair, he'd received a letter and he wanted to answer it in person, but he couldn't because he injured his ankle. He sent me with a cryptic message written in a book, and I walked into the drawing room of the Maison du Bois, and there was my mother. When I told you that I work for Lord Hazing, I used the wrong tense. I did work for him. I don't see myself going back to my desk and acting just as though I didn't know my mother was his ex-mistress."

"But Kerry —" Benjamin Drummond stopped abruptly. "Look, I need a drink. My head's turning circles."

A steward appeared.

"What's yours, Kerry?"

"Sherry, please."

"Sherry for the lovely lady, Joe, and the usual for me. Only this time, go easy on the rocks and don't spare the Scotch."

The man, grinning, withdrew, and Mr. Drummond put a question.

"Kerry, how much were you ever told about your father?"

"Why do you ask?"

"Because it shocks me, yes, that's the word, shocks me to think of your mother keeping back anything that you want to know. She told you nothing about me. If Pierre hadn't shown up, would you ever have known anything about him?"

"No. But she's written to my father to ask his permission to "

"Permission! For God's sake!"

"I know you'll find this bit hard to believe," Kerry told him, "but the one thing I was afraid of finding out was that one of the people she'd written to might be my father, and that he might be on his way here. I asked her, and she said it was quite certain that he wouldn't come. Something in the way she said it convinced me, and I relaxed."

"But hell, Kerry, isn't it time to shake the

moths out of the past?"

"You can't shake the moths out of someone else's past."

"If you want to know who your father is, she has no right to keep it from you."

"I think she's right to give him a chance to —"

"— to duck? I don't think she's right at all."

"If you'd turned out to be my father, would you have liked us, my sister Dale and me, to come up that gangway while you were at breakfast with your family, and claim you?"

"I'd be proud to own you. But all right," he conceded grudgingly. "I can see it might have its tricky side."

The drinks were brought and put before them, but for the first time in her knowledge of him, Mr. Drummond seemed unaware that they were there. He sat frowning, almost brooding, and she did not rouse him. When he spoke, he seemed to have lost something of his confident manner.

"What you've got to realize, Kerry," he said, "is that you're a totally different proposition from your mother. You've got a good head, and you can use it. You don't have to wait for your mother to make decisions. You've got a right to know anything you want to know."

"I wouldn't like to argue about rights, but I do know that I wouldn't like to try and prise out of her anything she doesn't want to give away."

"Would you like me to go back and talk with her?"

"No, thank you. I wouldn't. But as you've

filled up some gaps for me, I'd like to explain that she isn't as much of a fool as you think."

"I didn't say —"

"No, I know. But the others will be coming back at any moment, and I'd like to explain that in spite of everything that's happened to my mother since she left home, she's remained a Mostyn. She was born a Mostyn, and she's got all the Mostyn traits — the strongest of which is a complete lack of interest in anything that's happening in the world, anything that's taking place over the wall of the garden. They're completely self-contained; all they want is to be left to potter about doing their various jobs or hobbies. They don't mix, even with each other. My mother's like them. When she thought she was going to lose this house, she got into a panic, because in it she's back where she started, safe inside four walls, self-contained, content to live here even when all the summer people go. My aunts, who brought up my sister and myself, never knew who my father was, and I honestly think, didn't care. They'd understand why my mother wants to consult my father before telling me who he is — it's the Mostyn idea of individual freedom — he's free to keep to himself if he wants to. You probably know my mother a great deal better than I do, but in this one thing, I understand her better than I think you can."

He was silent for a time.

"That sounded like a summing-up for the defense," he said at last. "Are you feeling filial?"

"No. I just —"

"Nothing's simple, is it? You're trying to say that in keeping to their own remote little by-paths, your mother and your aunts show more good sense than most. Well, maybe they do, at that. The world's too full of sheep. The world's run by sheep, especially American sheep. Get out of line, and you're labelled a nut, a screwball — or worse. We've got group disease." He speared an olive angrily, put it into his mouth and threw toothpick and pit overboard with a gesture of fury. "Group disease. Fraternities and sororities and this club and that guild and circle and God knows how many let's-get-togethers and let's-hold-hands. I'm not complaining. I'm not a Mostyn. Maybe that's what I found so satisfying in your mother, her Mostyn blood. Shall we drink to that?"

She drank to it, but there was a kind of sickness within her for which she knew there was no cure. She wanted to have time to ply him with questions. He could tell her so much, and he had told her nothing. She was as sure now as she had been uncertain on the beach that he was holding something back. She knew that while he had been speaking, he had been debating whether he would or would not say what she was convinced he wanted to say, but he had ended by keeping it to himself. And apart from any natural curiosity that she or Dale might have concerning their father, they had no right to probe, to seek to know any more of their mother's past. She had come to Gaston-le-Grand and pushed open a door, but

214

there were, beyond it, other doors that were still closed and that she could not enter. She had learned much, but if there was a conspiracy of silence against her, there was no way she could defeat it. This man, Benjamin Drummond, might tell her more if she pressed him, but she would not press him, and she did not think that Dale would, either.

They sat in silence. Someone had opened the piano and was experimenting with its tinny tone. Benjamin Drummond offered her another drink, and she shook her head.

"No, thank you. I'm no good at drinking before lunch. I get swimmy."

"Then we'll eat. God knows why we're not eating now." She could feel his relief; he had been afraid of being questioned too closely. "We've got an army of cooks and waiters or stewards or crew or whatever, and look at the time, and you're sitting there slowly starving to death." He raised his voice in a yell. "Connie! Connie, come out here!"

His wife came on deck. Pierre was with her, but not the children.

"Food," her husband demanded. "We're sitting here and —"

"Patience, patience, Ben," she intoned. "It's ordered. It's coming. But I had to settle the kids first; I didn't want them to eat out here. They take food on their plates," she explained to Kerry, "and next thing, they're throwing it to the gulls."

Two stewards appeared, one pushing something that looked like a toy wheelbarrow, the other following with a folding table, which was put up and covered with a red-and-white checked cloth. The plates and knives and forks were laid on it, and cold and hot dishes were lifted from the wheelbarrow and placed beside them.

"All right, boys, thanks. I'll do the dishing out," Mr. Drummond said.

He piled plates, Pierre's highest of all. When they had finished, and had drunk their coffee, he offered to give the mural another look.

"I'm fine at business," he told Pierre, "but I'm low on culture. You come and show me what I should have seen in that painting. It's all a kind of gamble, it seems to me. I've got this friend who's been buying canvases with just one big blob of colour. 'What's that?' I asked him, and he said, 'Ben, I don't know, but the artist looked hungry.' And next thing, the blobs turn out to be the latest thing in syncopated realism, I think it was — or maybe realistic syncope, who cares? — and my friend was unloading them at a vast profit and all I can't tell you is whether the artist is still hungry or whether he's eating. Come on, Pierre. Teach me."

As they went inside, the deck resounded with the thumping of children's feet. Pete clamoured to return to the beach, and Mr. Drummond and Pierre came out in time to give a casting vote.

"You coming?" Jumbo asked Pierre.

"Certainly, but not so soon after my food."

"Why don't you come to dinner?" Jumbo asked eagerly. "Mom, he can come to dinner, can't he?"

"I am sorry," Pierre said, "but I must fetch my car back from Nantes. Then when I come back, I hope Kerry will dine with me in a restaurant owned by a friend of mine. He played the violin, but he could not make much money. So he opened this restaurant, and now he is rich. It is very sad."

"What — being rich?" asked Jumbo in surprise.

"No. It is sad that he gave up playing his violin."

"They say cooking's also an art," Connie said.

"He is not a cook."

"Oh, I thought you said —"

"No. His mother is the cook. It is his mother's house. It was his idea, certainly, to make it into a restaurant, but it is his mother who has made it famous with her cooking. Half the profits are hers, half are his."

"If it's a restaurant, boys can go, can't they?" Jumbo said.

"Boys? Small boys like you? No. Not for dinner," Pierre said firmly.

"I've seen small boys like me, French boys too, having dinner in restaurants," Jumbo stated.

"In family restaurants, certainly. This is allowed. But at night in this restaurant I am talking about, it is not for children. Only for older people. Your father and mother could go, but not tonight, because tonight they would not get a table. Tonight is the birthday of my friend Juan's mother, and he has arranged a surprise party for her."

"Juan? That's not French," commented Mr. Drummond.

"His mother, the cook, is Spanish," Pierre explained.

Jumbo turned to Kerry.

"You going to go with Pierre?" he asked her.

"I'll have to ask my mother first," Kerry replied, and was gratified at the three children's hysterical reception of what they took to be a joke.

Chapter Nine

The restaurant was called the Cours Bretagne, and stood at one end of a narrow, cobbled alley. The house, more Basque than Breton, was built around a flowery patio and must have looked charming when the lanterns were lit and the tables were gleaming with cutlery and crystal. But tonight, Pierre and Kerry found on their arrival, there were no lanterns and no gleam of any kind. And there was no dinner.

Seated in groups, looking gloomy, were about twenty men and women dressed informally but with touches here and there marking a festive occasion. One of the men greeted Pierre with a nod and jerked his chin upward.

"*Écoute*," he said.

From the upper story of the house was issuing a shrill stream of abuse. From time to time, a man's voice uttered a syllable or two, only to be shouted down. From the murmurs of the assembled guests, Kerry began to grasp the situation.

The party had certainly proved a surprise for Juan's mother. She was now inquiring who these guests were who were not her friends but his. What right had he, a partner in the business, to close its doors to paying customers without reference to her? Had she slaved all day to prepare food for this bunch of slovenly, no-good, un-washed, unshaven louts and their women? Did he realize how much money they would lose to-night? If this was her party, where were her friends? Where was old Père Rouleaux, and Emile, and Gauthier? And what of the regular customers who would come expecting a meal, to find themselves shut out? Would they return to-morrow? Certainly they would not. Would this make the fame of the restaurant spread, grow?

Pierre, tiring, lifted up his voice and shouted. The window opened and a swarthy, moustached face was thrust out — not Juan, as Kerry sup-posed, but Juan's mother, giving those below three minutes in which to disperse before she poured over their heads they well knew what. Juan? Let him out? Didn't they know it was his old mother's birthday, ha ha ha ha ha? Let him stay at home and keep her company.

The window closed with a crash. The com-pany dispersed.

"So," Pierre said, as he walked beside Kerry to his car. "The party is over."

"Poor Juan."

"Perhaps. But it is her restaurant as well as his. He should have asked some of her old cronies. I suppose you wish that you had stayed at home and dined with your mother?"

"She wasn't there. There was a message — she'd gone into Nantes with Monsieur Courbet. So where do we eat?"

"I don't know. If you want to know the truth, I

did not bring much money, thinking that we were to be guests. Now, of course, we shall have to pay."

"How much money did you bring?"

He stopped by the car and emptied his pockets and held out the total.

"Is that all you carry about with you?" she asked in surprise.

"If I don't expect to spend money, why should I carry more? How much have you got with you?"

"Thinking we were to be guests, I didn't bring much money."

There was a pause.

"We could go to the Drummonds on the yacht," he suggested. "They invited us."

"And we refused. At least, you did. Any other suggestions?"

"With only this money, we cannot dine like dukes, you understand? You would have to —"

"— lower my standards? Well, I'll do that, just for this evening. Now will you please take me somewhere where they're serving hungry customers?"

He drove her to the outskirts of the town, along a wide street flanked by handsome houses.

"The Boulevard Brousson," he said. "If Gaston-le-Grand has a founder, he is Brousson. Brousson opened the first shop and the first restaurant. He built the first house on this boulevard."

"Why didn't he choose a place with a view, like

221

the hill my mother's house is on?"

"When hardworking shopkeepers become rich, they do not want to look at a view or gaze at the sea. They build comfortable houses like these that you can see."

"Who owns the Villa Azul and the other one — Gabrielle?"

"Business people in Nantes. They never come. An agent does everything."

He turned into a narrower road, and ahead, Kerry saw the sea. Soon they came out on the road bordering the beach that she had seen hitherto only from a distance. He stopped at a small, unpretentious restaurant.

"You will perhaps not like this one," he said. "It is really for the beach attendants. But you will get food. Only one plate, but —"

"Tell me inside."

They entered a swing door and found themselves in a steamy room crowded to suffocation, the tables so close together that there was barely room to pass between them. At the end, behind a wide counter, three stout women and a white-hatted chef stood ladling food from enormous iron pots. Waiters in shirtsleeves carried brimming plates and by a miracle set them down before the diners without a drop spilled.

"Tonight, only stew," Pierre said, after eyeing a menu pinned on the wall. "Each night is only one thing; tonight, stew."

Kerry opened her mouth to say that under no circumstances whatever would she eat stew, when a waiter pushed by holding aloft two plates, leaving in his trail an odour so delicious that without further delay she began to push her way determinedly past bowed backs and busy elbows until she reached what appeared to be the last vacant table. Pierre, after a slight skirmish with the neighbours, wedged himself opposite. There was no ceremony. A passing waiter wiped the plastic-topped table. One of the women leaned over the counter and gave them glasses and a bottle of wine. The chef handed them battered knives and forks and two coarse but clean napkins. A basket with hunks of bread came next, and then two huge plates of stew.

The din precluded conversation, but they could eat. Kerry found that the food tasted even better than it had smelled. Pierre watched her as she wiped her plate clean with the last piece of bread but shook his head when she indicated that she would like a second helping; their money would not run to it.

He paid the bill and she followed him outside.

"You are still hungry?" he asked.

"No. But I could have eaten three more helpings of that so-called stew. It was wonderful."

"This is France. At even a poor-looking restaurant, you can get superb food. You can even —"

"What are you shivering for?"

He got into the car and put up the collar of his jacket.

"Why do people shiver? Because they are cold.

223

In there, it was like a furnace. Now perhaps I shall catch a chill; often, I do. Will you come down to the beach? There is a moon, we can walk on the sand and I shall get warm."

They went down, but instead of walking, sat in the shelter of the sea wall.

"That is better," Pierre said. "Now I shall get warm. Later, when people have finished dining, they will come here and walk about and it will become crowded. Many people are having holidays."

"Is that what you were doing in the Dordogne — having a holiday?"

"I went to visit a friend of mine — an artist, a woman. She is going to England, to have an exhibition of her work in London. Perhaps when you go back, you will go and see it?"

"I don't get much time for going round exhibitions."

"Then you should do some other kind of work."

"You don't understand. I work for tycoons. I'm not sure what a tycoon is, but I think it's the type that got rich by trampling their competitors in the dust. They're hard to work for, but they pay well. In a few years, I've actually saved money — real money in a real bank."

"You like money so much?"

"I like feeling independent. I like spending money I've earned myself. My aunts won't take any of it, so I put what I don't need into the bank. I work long, hard, erratic hours. I suppose it's a sort of slavery, but it's also a shortcut to being able to buy a car, which I don't need, or a flat, which I do. I work off all my tension, as I told you, in exercising, one way or another. It's hard on my men friends, most of whom get tired and drop out, but so far, I haven't missed them. Nobody's ever given me a bigger thrill than the one I got the first time I beat the club coach at tennis."

"It seems a strange ambition for a girl as attractive as you, to beat the club coach. When you go back, will you return to this man who sent you with the message to your mother?"

"No. Could you? Could anyone? No."

"You will go to another tycoon?"

"I suppose so. Pierre —"

"That is the first time you have said my name. It is not the right way to say it, but I shall not correct you because you make it sound — different."

"I wanted to ask you something. You know that while you were looking at the mural on board after lunch, I —"

"You were on deck with Mr. Drummond. Yes. And you spoke about your mother. You also spoke about my father."

"Did he tell you that —"

"— that it was my father who, shall we say, took your mother from him? He did not have to tell me. I can do arithmetic and I can work some things out for myself."

"Did you get the impression that he — Mr.

225

Drummond — knew a lot more than he was giving away?"

"No."

"Well, I did."

"And that is why you were not gay, not happy when we left the yacht? Because you wanted to know more about your mother's past?"

"Not really. If I said it wasn't all a bit baffling, frustrating, then of course I'd be a liar. But I knew, when I was talking to him, that there were things he could tell me if I asked. Only — I couldn't ask. The Professor — I couldn't have learned much from him. I could from Mr. Drummond. I don't believe he'd live for three years with a woman without getting a pretty accurate picture of her life. He's not the kind of man who'd let her sit on all her secrets, as she's done with me. And as I said, I don't want to ask too much, but it's all there, in a sort of tangle, and it would be interesting to unravel it. Take that Miss Arran-Duff, for example. She said quite clearly, to you and me, that this was the first time she'd been here. But my mother knew her, years ago. And I can't ask Miss Arran-Duff where or when. So you see?"

"Yes, I see."

"Then let's forget my mother and talk about something else. About you. Let's drag out all the facts about your life."

"You know about my life. I am a painter. Of course, you do not go to exhibitions, so you have not seen any of my work. I think you are the first person I have met who knows my father hardly at all. Only a few years ago, he conducted all the greatest works, all the greatest players, all the greatest orchestras. The concert halls were full, the applause — you should have heard it. Today, this happens when he is a guest conductor. And all the time, what are you doing? Swimming. To swim is good, but how can you live without music? Listen to me, please. I am going to buy you some of my father's recordings to show you what you have missed, what you are missing. You shall hear the works of artists who have spent their lives perfecting their art, who have lived for their art. If you will come to Paris, I will fish your poor little starved soul out of its swimming pool and feed it with glorious sound. I will —"

"We weren't talking about me. We were talking about you. Isn't there anything you do that can be said to be healthy, outdoor, strenuous or even active?"

"Yes. Sometimes I sail."

"Sail?"

"Last year, I bought a little boat. I learned how to sail it. I keep it at St. Malo. That is how I know the yacht that the Drummonds have hired, since that is also kept at St. Malo."

"You learned sailing, but you didn't learn how to swim first?"

"Always when I sail the little boat, I wear a jacket, a life-jacket to keep me from sinking if I fall into the sea. If you come over from England, perhaps you will come for a sail with me. I also thought of another idea when you told me that you were not going back to work for the man who sent you here: that instead of working in London, you should work in Paris. In this way you would improve or even perfect your French and you would also see the work that I do. I shall be honest and tell you that this idea first came not from me, but from Mr. Drummond."

"What on earth has it got to do with him?"

"He was worried about you because your mother told you so little about the facts of her life. He thinks this is wrong."

"Then why didn't he supply a few facts himself? He sat there on the deck testing every word he spoke, before he uttered it, in case he gave anything away."

"Because he thought he had no right to interfere. He is going away tomorrow and perhaps will never see you or your mother again; he told me that although he thinks it wrong, if not wicked to conceal the past from you, he does not see how he can go against your mother's wish to preserve her secrets."

"Did she ask him to preserve her secrets?"

"Yes. But she did not tell him frankly how much, how little you knew. When you talked to him, he was shocked."

"Not shocked enough to give anything away," she said regretfully.

After this exchange, neither of them spoke until Kerry suggested that it was time to move.

When they were nearing the car, they saw two people seated in it.

"The Drummonds," Kerry said. "And if they ask me to go aboard and have a drink, I'm going to. How about you?"

"For a drink, no. But they will perhaps give us sandwiches."

Mr. Drummond hailed them.

"You've been a long time. We came out for an airing, and then we saw the car and decided to wait for you. Come on back to the boat and let's all have a drink."

"And in case you're thinking of refusing," his wife added, "the kids are all safely in bed and won't bother you."

They drove to the quay. Through the window of the hut they could see the official, still wearing his peaked cap, warm and comfortable beside the remains of his meal, his snores clearly audible.

"I'm going to apply for that job when I get too old to work," Mr. Drummond remarked. "Does he stay on so-called duty all night?"

"No. At midnight, another man comes," Pierre said. "At ten o'clock tomorrow morning, this man returns. This is the same man I remember from a boy; he used to let me take the dinghy and kept watch to warn me if my mother should come."

"Oh, one of those mothers?" Mr. Drummond said. "There's only one cure for that kind: just put them in charge of our three kids for a week.

That's right, isn't it, Connie?"

"That's right," she agreed. "When they were little, I started off by saying they couldn't do this and they shouldn't do that, and then one day I got to realize that they'd all turned stone deaf. So I quit."

"And there you have the great American problem," Mr. Drummond drawled. "The kids wouldn't listen to orders, so Mom stopped giving 'em."

"Not American, universal," Pierre remarked. "That is, when there is more than one child. With one child, the mother can impose her will."

"Only if the child's meek and mild, as you appear to have been," Kerry told him.

He made no reply; he was preparing to row them to the yacht. They were soon seated on the deep, comfortable settees in the saloon, the much discussed mural scarcely visible in the soft lighting. Through one of the portholes, Kerry could see the quay and the little hut. Above was the dark, pine-clad hillside and, when the breeze stirred the branches, a winking light from the houses on the hill.

"Look." Mr. Drummond, having ordered drinks and sandwiches, addressed Kerry. "I've got an idea."

"Me, too," said his wife. "Why don't we persuade Pierre and Kerry to sail back to St. Malo with us?"

"That's what she's always doing," Mr. Drummond complained. "I get a good idea, she guesses what it is and gets in first and claims it. All right, so she's made the proposition. How about it?"

"You are very kind. But for me, it is impossible," Pierre said. "And for Kerry, too."

"Can he speak for you?" Mr. Drummond asked Kerry.

"I can say this much for her, that I am sure she is not thinking of leaving so soon. She has only just met her mother. Can she run away after just a few days?"

"No, she can't," Kerry said.

"Well, that's a pity." Mr. Drummond sounded genuinely disappointed. "If you'd been coming, I could've waited another day, but I only hired this thing for a short cruise, and I thought it would be a good idea to leave tomorrow and poke around a few little ports on the way back." His gaze went to the mural. "It's funny how you turned out to be a painter," he said musingly. "The way you handled the kids' choir on the beach, I'd have thought music would've been your line."

"A painter," said Pierre, "or —"

"Wait for it," Kerry warned the Drummonds. "He's now going to claim to be equally good at all the arts, to say nothing of all the sports. If he hadn't been a famous painter, he would have been a famous musician, taking time off to swim in the Olympics."

"All the same, his father was one of the greats," Mr. Drummond said. "I went to one of his concerts once, and I still remember him. And not only for his conducting." His eyes met those of his wife, and he laughed, a sound compounded of amusement, ruefulness and a kind of small-boy mischief that brought an answering smile to her lips. "I'll confess, Connie. I took a woman with me, and that was a big mistake. She was beautiful, but so was this conductor."

"Beautiful, no," Pierre said. "He was —"

"Quiet," admonished Kerry. "Please go on, Mr. Drummond."

"Well, Connie, there it was. She was beautiful, and in spite of what Pierre was going to say, his father was beautiful too. Why can't a man be beautiful? If he's got a splendid head, a fine body, what they call chiselled features, good limbs, then why can't you call him beautiful?"

"All right, so he was beautiful," Connie allowed. "So what happened? You lost your lady friend?"

"Not that evening. But that's when it all began. Maybe if I'd acted real quick, taken up the violin or the flute —"

"You should have taken up your lady friend and got her out of Paris, if that's where you were," Connie said. "Come to think of it, maybe that's why you moved so fast that time in Austria, when I said I liked the look of that skiing instructor. All I said," she told Pierre and Kerry, "was that he was big and strong and gave me a feeling of confidence. And the next thing, Ben had decided there wasn't enough sunshine in that part of the mountain, and we'd move on. I guess he was taking no chances. Hey, Ben, look: four empty glasses."

Mr. Drummond would have refilled them, but Kerry thought it was time to go.

"Will you come down to the beach tomorrow for a picnic lunch?" Connie asked. "We'll be sailing right afterward, but you've got to say goodbye to the kids. How are we going to get Jumbo to come with us and leave Pierre behind?"

"We are going to meet soon in Paris," Pierre pointed out.

He rowed Kerry back to the quay and then drove her to the Maison du Bois. He stopped the car at the wicker gate, but made no move to get out.

"Tomorrow," he said, "I am going to move to the Villa Leclair."

"The hostel? Why?" Kerry asked in surprise.

"Because I took my room at the hotel for two days only. Now they need it, so I must go. I would have moved in any case to the hostel, because I want to paint. I want very much to paint your portrait. Will you let me?"

"How long does it take to paint somebody's portrait?"

"How long are you going to stay with your mother?"

"Not for very long. Are you free to stay as long as you want to?"

"I shall stay as long as you stay."

233

"Do I get the portrait when you've painted it?"

"But no, certainly not." He sounded astonished. "The portrait will be mine. I shall exhibit it."

"Sell it to some stranger, you mean?"

"Sell? No. I said exhibit. Then I shall keep it in my apartment."

"Do you think anybody ever painted my mother's portrait?"

"She would not be as interesting as you to paint. I would not paint her. I am glad that you do not look like her. Certainly you are not like her in other ways. You would not behave as she has behaved."

"How do you know?"

"How does any man know?"

"Well, tell me."

"It is not possible to explain, to define. There is a look. You have not got it. Your mother has, clearly. I do not mean that she seeks to attract men; women like her do not have to seek. I mean only that there is beauty you can possess, and beauty you cannot possess. I would not paint your mother, but I would like very much to paint you."

"Do you paint many of the women you meet?"

"No, I do not."

"Only the outstanding ones?"

"Who is boasting now?"

"I am. Why can't I have the portrait when it's finished?"

"The work of an artist —"

"— can be commissioned. But if you're as famous as I'm beginning to believe, I couldn't pay your fee. How about a small-size profile? A profile's only half a face, and I could pay you in installments. Nobody's ever likely to approach me again with an easel and brushes under his arm, so I hate to go away and leave my painted self behind. What happens after you've hung me up, I mean hung me in your apartment?"

"At any time, you can come and look at it."

"How much time am I likely to have for that? I've got to get back and look for another job. But I'll spread the word, and when you've got tired of having a stream of strangers asking to have a look at it, perhaps you'll make me a present of it."

"It would depend."

"On what? Collateral? You've just told me that there's a look, and I haven't got it. So what does it depend on?"

"On whether I could look at you in the flesh."

"Explain, Leclair. Explain, or modify."

"It is simple. Why do I want to paint your portrait? Because I wish to see you when you are not with me. If you are with me, I do not need the portrait."

"If I'm with you, I shan't need the portrait either; it'll be there on the wall in front of me. Are you trying to say something?"

"Yes. But you do not make it easy. You make things into a joke. Some things cannot be made into jokes. This, for instance: that I am going to paint your portrait and in this way insure that

235

whatever happens, I shall not lose you."

There was a long silence. Out of it came at last Kerry's softly spoken, astounded comment

"Well, I'll be — I'll be —"

"I do not know why you should be so surprised. Why did I not go at once, back to Paris?"

"Because you wanted to hear the quartet, that's why."

"And when two of the four went away, what then? You saw them go. So what kept me? You should have asked yourself."

"I would have given myself the wrong answer."

"Why? I am not handsome. I am not perhaps like all these other fat men you know, but you do not have to be fat and handsome to fall in love. You should have guessed."

"How could I guess? There's a look, and you haven't got it. There's a manner, too, and you haven't got that either. Besides a look and a manner, there's a method, but you don't seem to have grasped it. A man who claims to have fallen in love doesn't sit down in front of an easel and —"

"Certainly he does. If he is an artist, certainly he does. How else shall a painter express himself? If a man is a poet, he writes verses. A musician will compose a nocturne, a symphony. If a man has no creative ability, all that is left for him is to speak, but speech is not so expressive as music or a poem or a painting. Also, what is there to say after so short an acquaintance? A man has to wait. A man has to be sure that he has not mistaken his feelings."

"Oh, really?"

"Certainly. If you go too fast, you fall."

"I thought you'd already fallen."

"I have to consider. I have to pause. I have to say to myself: Is this rash? What, I have to ask myself, does one know of a person after only two, three days?"

"What, indeed?"

"What value can a declaration have, if it is to be unsaid later? What compliment is it to a woman to hear that, knowing nothing whatsoever about her, a man loves her? Can it be for her intelligence, her kindness, her faithfulness, her stability, her talents? No, because he knows nothing of these things. It can only be because he is struck by her looks, and what are looks? Certainly in this case you cannot be struck by my looks, and so I must offer something more, my gifts. If you find that I deserve my early fame as an artist, if you begin to see the man I am under my not-handsome exterior, then I can hope to impress you. Until then, I do not wish to. I believe that time is needed for life's patterns to be worked out. All my life I have learned this, through my father, perhaps even through your mother. Their example was how I could see that by waiting, things would resolve themselves. For years I waited, my mother waited, and then my father was with us again. You are in London, I am in Paris, but if there is anything to draw us together, we shall come together. I will go to see your sister and your aunts, and you will come to Paris to meet my parents and my friends." He stopped. "There is only one thing that I should like to know, and that is whether you have ever been in love with somebody."

"No."

"But men have loved you. That one who wished to show you the châteaux, and I suppose others too." He sounded bitter. "Did they make declarations?"

"They didn't ask me to wait until they dashed off a poem or a nocturne. One way and another, it looks to me as though you've got a busy time in front of you: French lessons, swimming lessons, painting my portrait and pondering on your future."

"Our future."

"Yours. I've merely been auditioned and I'm being considered for the part."

"You are angry."

"I'm full of admiration. I've never met a man with your kind of courage."

"Yes, you are angry. But Kerry —"

But she was getting out of the car.

"Tell me tomorrow, when my head's clearer," she said. "My mother's light is still on; I'm going to ask her how long your father pondered before snatching her away from Benjamin Drummond."

"Kerry —"

She did not turn. She went into the house and closed the door. As she went up the stairs, her mother called to her, and she went into the room. Her mother was sitting up in bed, and Kerry studied her for a moment. Halo of light from the bedside table, soft white lace covering the blankets, soft pink silk bedjacket over soft pink silk nightdress. And an incongruous, disarming, perhaps honest Mostyn touch: hair set and held by clips and tied with a net scarf.

"I'm sorry I didn't come back to have dinner with you, Kerry. But in any case, you were dining out."

"I wouldn't have gone if you'd been here."

"Did you go with Pierre Leclair?"

"Yes. We had drinks afterward on the Drummonds' boat. They asked us if we'd like to go back to St. Malo with them."

"But they go tomorrow. That's too soon."

"Yes. But I'm afraid I shan't be able to stay very much longer."

Did her mother, she wondered, think she was going back to work for Lord Hazing? Did she think that her daughter had no curiosity about the past? Was there ever going to be a word said between them that was intimate, affectionate?

"Kerry —"

"Yes?"

Madame Daumier shook her head.

"It's no use," she said disarmingly. "I try to say things that sound motherly, but they won't come out."

"I'd stop trying if I were you," Kerry said gently.

"You're just what I'd like a daughter of mine to be, if I felt like a mother — but I don't."

"Don't you want to meet Dale?"

"Yes. I want to see in what way she looks like me. But if I had to do things all over again, I'd do the same as I did before, leave you both with your aunts. But I suppose that makes you feel resentful."

"No, it doesn't. But you needn't have asked Mr. Drummond to say nothing about — well, about anything. I wouldn't have tried to get it out of him. Aren't you going to feel lonely here when we've all gone?"

"No. Edouard Courbet goes about a good deal, and he knows some interesting people, like the ones we dined with tonight. He'll take me to Paris whenever I want to go."

"Is the sale of the house completed?"

"Yes. His lawyers have got all the papers. And he's made arrangements for the sale of my pearls, so you see, everything has worked out very well. I shall have to go into Nantes tomorrow to sign things. Will you mind having lunch by yourself?"

"The Drummonds asked me to a picnic lunch on the beach."

"That's all right, then."

Her mother adjusted the pillows. Her hand went to the light switch. Kerry stood for a moment fighting the sudden rush of anger, frustration, contempt, pity, yearning to uncover the past that threatened to overwhelm her. Then the confusion passed, and something totally unexpected took its place. Soft as was the light that shone by her mother's bed, it showed Kerry for the first time the answer to the problem that had baffled her ever since her arrival at the Maison du Bois: how her mother could have attracted and held men as able, as diverse, as brilliant as Lord Hazing and the Professor and Pierre's father and Benjamin Drummond. She had known that sex was not the whole answer, but that was all she had known. Now she saw that in her mother's beauty there was a quality of sadness, something that for want of a better word she termed *wistfulness*. The blue eyes had a lost, waiflike appeal, and seeing it now, Kerry felt that it was easy to understand the protective response it would rouse in a strong man. And after that? Her infinite restfulness. She was a fool, but it was a negative and not a jarring foolishness. The men who had loved her had not been seeking mental companionship. Busy, creative, they had spent themselves and turned to her for the one thing they needed: peace. In her soft, soothing, undemanding presence they sought and found renewal. She did not provide and they did not need stimulation; they required no more than a refuge from the pressures of their working lives.

The thoughts passed, but a feeling of lightness remained; at last she felt that she had a clear picture to show Dale. But there was nothing she could say to her mother. There was nothing to do but wish her goodnight and go quietly out of the room. You could only fight, she told herself, throwing her shutters open and staring out into the night, you could only fight if there were something to fight against. Her mother lived in the present. She had dropped the past like a discarded garment, and there was no hope of persuading her to pick it up and shake it. She had grown up alone; she had turned her back on Orchard House and its inmates, gone away and left them so far behind that they were now no more than dim figures in a past she had no desire to revive. Her father, her sisters, her children, the men she had known — these were milestones marking her progress, and as they dropped behind, she forgot them.

Kerry undressed and got into bed. Was it the maternal urge that was the strongest of all? No. There was one even stronger: self-preservation. Madame Daumier, she thought, was very well preserved.

But it was not of her mother that she was thinking as she fell asleep. Her thoughts were purely culinary; they were of starches, peanut butter, good, thick soups, great thick hunks of bread, sugar, cream . . .

Chapter Ten

There was almost a crowd on the beach the next morning, but the juvenile element, though out in strength, was still not strong enough to hold off Jumbo Drummond, who after a highly successful series of raids, was in possession of three brand-new beach balls, three inflated rubber animals and an Indian canoe. Laden with booty, he was for once disposed to share with Pete and Priss, and the three could be seen riding the waves in triumph while their mother turned a deaf ear to complaints in three languages, savage looks and threats of reprisal. Of Mr. Drummond there was no sign, but Pierre was in bathing trunks at the edge of the sea, summoning courage to go in and assuring Jumbo that it was not necessary to hold the canoe in readiness for a rescue.

Kerry joined them, and the swimming lesson began. At the end of it, Pierre surveyed the beach and announced that there were enough children to form a grand choir. The word was no sooner spoken than Jumbo began a roundup, uttering threats that made parents' blood curdle and herding the victims into a line and parading them before Pierre.

"Twenty-two," he announced. "But I bet they can't sing for peanuts."

They sang, under Pierre's baton, in a manner that drew a crowd. Mr. Drummond, arriving for the final item, a gay piece called "Chantez, Chantez, Coq-Coq-Coq," waited until the choir was dismissed and then addressed the conductor admiringly.

"But man, you kill me," he ended. "All this, and you don't even take around a hat. You'd make a killing! Then you could hand out cards: singing classes at so much a time. They'd flock!"

"They flock in Paris," Pierre said, walking toward the tent. "One day, if I do not sell my pictures, I shall take your advice." He stopped and gazed in astonishment at the four hampers lined up beside Connie. "All this is food?"

"Of course not. Half of it is drink," Connie told him. "It took three of the crew to get it here, while you were conducting. Go on in and put some clothes on, you look blue. And hurry. We're all hungry."

It was more a feast than a picnic, but Jumbo did not share the general high spirits. He ate little, and Kerry knew that he was fighting tears. They were to sail in an hour, and although he had Pierre's Paris address tucked securely into the belt of his swimming trunks and knew that they would meet again, a parting was still a parting.

Pierre and Kerry walked to the quay to see the family off. They watched them until they reached the yacht and were lined up on the deck, waving farewells. Then they went back to the tent and collected their towels. They were to pick up Pierre's luggage at the hotel and take it out to the hostel.

"Take me to the Maison du Bois first," Kerry requested. "I'll leave these wet things and change into a pair of slacks."

"Slacks?"

"Pants. Last time I went out to the Villa Leclair, I had to walk back."

He drove her to the house and waited in the drawing room until she had changed. Walking to the car, he stopped to inspect the neat gap that had been made in the hedge separating the garden from Monsieur Courbet's.

"That was not there in our time," he commented.

Kerry did not think that it had been there in Madame Courbet's time either, but she did not say so. They drove to the hotel, and she found it looking livelier than she had ever seen it; the season, such as it was, had obviously begun. She thought of the Professor with a pang. Perhaps he was now united with his daughter; he was certainly forgotten by her mother. She hoped he was happy.

Pierre paid his bill, and a bell on the counter was thumped to summon a boy to carry down his suitcase. No boy appeared, and Pierre decided to fetch it himself and went with long bounds up the creaky stairs, disdaining the creakier lift. Kerry stood idly by the reception counter, watching without much interest the coming and

245

going of visitors, who were assisted by burly porters and small boys too busy pocketing tips to answer bells. One of them, not much bigger than Jumbo, was carrying in the lighter articles of an old lady's luggage and getting in the way of his colleagues, who were hurrying out of the building in response to the loud summons of a newly arrived taxi.

Perhaps it was the attitude of those who stood around the taxi driver awaiting the alighting passenger — an attitude she saw every day in the office in London — subservient, cringing, eager to please, anxious not to bring down the terrible wrath of the master. Perhaps it was this, Kerry thought afterward, that first penetrated her consciousness. She was never to be entirely sure. It might have been the roar proceeding from the taxi's interior. It might even have been something vaguely familiar about the two expensive suitcases and the briefcase. But even if, much later, she was to recall these details, she was aware at this moment of nothing but a sense of disaster, inexplicable but paralyzing. Tense, she stared out at the street. And enlightenment came in the form of an out-thrust, plaster-encased ankle. Confirmation came with the sight of the broad, powerful body. Certainty reached her when she heard the stream of abuse directed at a hapless attendant who had mishandled the job of handing over the pair of crutches.

He had come, after all. He was here.

As she fought to disbelieve the evidence of her

eyes and ears, she wondered how she could ever have thought that he would not come. He had not known how long he would be disabled, and he had sent her to insure that his would be the first response to Madame Daumier's appeal. Of all the men to whom she had written, he alone had realized that he would not be the only one to whom she would turn. He had sent her what she wanted, by the swiftest possible method. And now he had come himself, not, she thought, for reward but because he never gave away anything without supervising the uses to which his gifts were put. He might be too late to supervise the purchase of Monsieur Courbet's house, but he was not too late to give his opinion as to its value.

He was here, and Kerry realized that with his arrival, her own stay was at an end. She had been living in a dream, but reality was here, at the door. He would now learn what she had determined that he would never learn from her: that his message had been sent to her mother. Her mother would tell him the truth, but before he learned it, she would be out of Gaston-le-Grand. There was no hesitation in her mind. She was going. The means to take her away were at hand, if only she could be in time.

She could not think clearly, but she knew that she was performing certain automatic actions. She had spoken to the receptionist, asking him to tell Monsieur Leclair that she had been called away. She had moved across the hall to the shelter of the tall plants in the corner by the door. As the procession entered, she could not be seen. The attendants hovered attentively; in their midst, Lord Hazing proceeded, using the crutches both as support and to clear the way. As he turned toward the reception counter, she slipped swiftly out to the street. Stopping and getting into the taxi, which had been about to drive away, she leaned back on the seat and struggled to find reasons for her desperate desire for flight but could produce from the confusion in her mind only the one certain fact that she could not, knowing what she knew, meet Lord Hazing and her mother together. They were free to meet or to part, she did not care which. All she knew was that she did not want to be linked with them. She had made her own life. She had not enjoyed working for Lord Hazing, but she had been proud of her ability to maintain, month after month, a calm façade through which he had never succeeded in breaking. Neither pride nor calmness would be possible if she came face to face with him at the Maison du Bois.

The taxi seemed to crawl, especially up the last, steep part of the journey to the house. When at last it stopped at the wicker gate, she told the man to wait and rushed into the hall, thankful to know that her mother would not be there. There was only Clothilde, and Kerry called to her as she ran up the stairs. As she packed, throwing garments from cupboards and drawers into the suitcase, she managed to make the woman understand that she had been called away. A few lines scrawled on a sheet of paper sufficed for her mother. Then Clothilde, bewildered, agitated, carried the suitcase out to the taxi, and Kerry got into it and gave orders to the driver.

"*Bateau.*" She waved a hand in the direction of the harbour. "*Bateau. Vite, vite!*"

For Pierre, she could leave no message save the one he would get from the hotel receptionist: she had gone. He would not understand, and she could not wait to explain. But he had said — hadn't he? — that if there was anything to draw them together, they would come together. She had not known, when he spoke, how much she had wanted to be drawn. She knew now, only too well.

The taxi driver, conscious at last of the need for speed, drove recklessly down the hill, rounded the curve on two wheels and missed the rocky edge by inches. But Kerry thought only of the moment when they would emerge onto the sea road and she would be able to see the harbour.

And then she saw it, and saw the large white yacht — and saw that it was moving. And perhaps it was her moan of despair, and her white, stricken face as they drew up at the quay, that lit in the driver's calloused heart a flame of chivalry; for it was he who glanced inside the hut, found the guardian slumbering and punched him awake. It was he who pushed the official and passenger into the little boat, threw in Kerry's luggage, pushed the boat out and then stood yelling, dancing, gesticulating until those on the yacht understood what he was trying to convey. Along the deck railing Kerry saw the Drummonds appear one by one. The distance between large and small craft lessened and at last closed. Standing at last in the rocking boat, Kerry reached out and grasped Benjamin's hand. She did not know what she said to him, but perhaps there had been no need to say anything; to the excited screams of the children, he helped Kerry aboard.

"Th-thanks." She was stammering breathlessly. "Can I c-come with you?"

"Sure, sure, sure." He spoke soothingly. "You're aboard, aren't you? Here's Connie."

At sight of Kerry's pallor, Connie spoke indignantly.

"Who's been frightening you?" she asked. "You just tell me, and I'll fix 'em."

"Nobody. It's nothing. I just — do you mind —"

"You come and sit in this chair and I'll have your grip taken along to your room, your cabin, your stateroom. But before you go after it, I'm going to give you a nice, strong drink. Look, you kids, get back, will you?"

"Where's Pierre?" Jumbo demanded. "Why didn't he come too?"

"I couldn't stop to tell him where I was going, Jumbo. It all happened rather suddenly. I — I remembered I had to get back to London, and I thought that if I could go with you —"

"Here. Stop talking and drink this," Benjamin ordered. "That'll make you feel better."

She was already feeling better, grateful beyond words for their warmth and kindness. Shock and disappointment were slipping away. She could almost argue herself back to her normal frame of mind. Why should the sight of the hill and the harbour, now beginning imperceptibly to recede, fill her mind with a kind of despair? What was she leaving? A house in which she had no interest and a mother who had no interest in her. Pierre Leclair, who was to have painted her portrait. Perhaps this strange, hollow feeling was the beginning of seasickness.

The trees on the hill seemed to be wavering. She put up a hand to her eyes and to her horror realized that she was weeping. Benjamin Drummond gently took away her untouched drink, Connie put a handkerchief into her hand and the three children stood transfixed, staring.

"I'm — I'm so sorry," Kerry sobbed. "I'm — I'm just behaving like a fool."

"You'll come and rest," Connie said firmly. "I always feel this way before a sea trip. I'm fine once we get started, but before takeoff, something gets into me, I can't tell you what, and I have to howl just like you're doing. Go ahead and get it out of your system."

"Why're you crying?" Jumbo asked.

"I'm not." She wiped her eyes firmly. "I was, but I've stopped. I was just being —"

She was interrupted by a terrible scream from Pete. For a moment Kerry thought — and saw that his mother and father thought — that he had gone overboard. Then they saw that he and Priss were hanging perilously over the railing, inarticulate with excitement, pointing shoreward. In a single movement, the others reached the railing. In dead silence they stood watching the scene unfolding between them and the shore.

Across the widening strip of water, they saw proceeding at reckless speed along the sea road, Pierre Leclair's car. The scream of brakes as it stopped at the quay was clearly audible. The door flew open, Pierre fell out, recovered and reached behind him for his suitcase. Clutching it, he went toward the rowing boat, and the official came hurrying out of the hut, obviously bent on preventing him from getting into it. Pierre's intention was clear: to row out to the yacht. The official's intention was also clear: to prove that the vessel was too far out; it too late to stop it.

The next moment, Pierre stepped to the end of the quay, threw his case into the boat, leaped in and grasped the oars. The yells of the official floated over the water; Pierre rowed steadily on. There was a wild shriek from Jumbo.

"He's coming with us! Dad, Mom, stop! He's coming with us! I knew he would, I knew it, I knew it! Aw, stop, can't you, Dad? Pierre! Pierre!"

"First stop St. Malo," yelled Pete.

"Gangway down, passengers up!" screamed Priss.

"Come on, Pierre!" Jumbo was hoarse and croaking. "Row, man, row!"

Pierre needed no urging. He was rowing desperately, the need for speed making him ignore all navigational hazards.

"Hold it!" Benjamin shouted in terror. "Look where you're going!" His voice dropped to a worried mutter. "The guy's crazy. Where the hell does he think he's going?"

There had been no orders, but the engines were beating with a slower rhythm. The yacht was slowing down. The little boat was within hail.

"Kerry! Kerry!" Pierre bent to the oars and brought the boat dangerously near the yacht. "Kerry, wait!"

Benjamin cupped his hands and shouted.

"Pierre, keep away! Mind that propeller. Pierre, d'you hear me?"

"Wait! I have got my baggage. Wait for me!" Pierre called.

He stood up. For a few wild moments, he managed to keep his balance — and then the wash from the yacht struck the little boat and sent it seesawing. Pierre swayed, recovered, gave a lurch and stumbled to one side. Slowly, gently, the little boat overturned.

"Oh, my God!" Benjamin groaned. "Will you look at that?" He was at the nearest lifebelt, unfastening it. "Get out of the way, you kids!" He sent it hurtling overboard, and it dropped with a thump near the surfacing Pierre, who began a desperate dog paddle toward it.

"Go on — grab it!" Benjamin shouted. "Grab it!"

253

Pierre sank. The suitcase, which had been floating beside him, followed him down into the depths. Then Pierre's head reappeared.

"Swim, man, swim!" Benjamin yelled.

Jumbo gave a desperate, choking cry.

Kerry did not hear it. She had kicked off her shoes and, poised for a moment on the rail, went over the side in a straight, clean dive. When she surfaced, she was on one side of Pierre. Jumbo was on the other. Between them, Pierre sank.

They dived for him, got his arms and hooked them around the lifebelt, holding it firm, waiting and watching as he gulped, choked and coughed in an effort to get his breath. At last he gave a long, noisy croak, put up a hand to push the hair out of his eyes and looked at Kerry.

"Kerry, I —"

"Hang onto the lifebelt," she told him.

On her back, one hand grasping the lifebelt, she swam away from the yacht, giving the propeller a wide berth as she swam to the other side, on which the gangway was once again being lowered. Jumbo swam beside Pierre, grasping his arms firmly.

Benjamin helped them aboard. On the deck, Connie was waiting with blankets for Kerry, for Jumbo and for Pierre.

"Get Pierre downstairs and get his clothes off," she told her husband. "I'll get hot drinks. Kerry, come with me. Jumbo, go along to your cabin and strip."

For once, Jumbo obeyed. When Kerry,

changed and dry, went along the narrow corridor and stopped at Benjamin's cabin door, she saw Pierre in his host's clothes and the entire family grouped around him, anxiously waiting for him to stop shaking.

"Give him another blanket and get him up on deck in the sun," ordered Benjamin. "When're those drinks coming, Connie, for God's sake? I could've boiled a gallon of liquid by now. Get 'em moving, will you? Run along, kids. Leave Pierre alone till he's got his circulation back. Wait a minute, Pierre, I've got a thicker sweater you can put on. It's on deck. I'll get it."

The children had not moved. Pierre, still shaking, was talking to Kerry.

"Kerry, it was wrong to run away. You —"

"I'll explain later," she said. "Stop talking, and then your teeth won't chatter."

"Here." Connie entered with a tray on which were three steaming tumblers. "Drink this, Pierre. Kerry, here's yours. Jumbo, get this down you and be careful, don't burn your tongue; it's hot, and I mean hot. Ben, do you have to come in? We're crowding Pierre and — oh, a thicker sweater. Good. Pierre, put it on."

He struggled into it. He was already wearing blue linen trousers that were too short, a cotton shirt that was too large and a sweater from which his neck stuck out like that of a molting swan.

"Come up on deck," Benjamin urged. "The sun's hot."

"First," Pierre said, "I must speak with Kerry about something."

"Then we'll leave you to get it said," Connie told him, and drove the family out like a flock of geese. Pierre was at last free to say what he seemed so anxious to say.

"Kerry, you should have waited."

"I couldn't. Finish your drink."

"It is too hot. I came downstairs from my room with my luggage and the man told me you had gone. I asked him why, and he said he didn't know, but when I looked round, then I knew at once. But it was foolish of you to act without thinking. Naturally, it was a shock; this is what I told him. I said that he should have prepared you, he and your mother between them. I said I could not stay to speak with him, because I was thinking about how you would go away, and I remembered this ship and I guessed you would try to catch it up. He seemed to feel too much to be able to speak, but —"

"I don't know what you're talking about," Kerry said. But a cold feeling that had nothing to do with the recent immersion was creeping over her. "Will you drink that up?"

"I am warm. I am simply saying that it was childish to run away. What I do not know, is how he came so soon. I think she did not write; she must have telephoned. Or perhaps she did nothing and he came as those other men came, to see her. But for you to be there, for you to see him, face him, recognize him at last and then run away — You are pale. You are not cold?"

"No."

"Shall we go on deck?"

"No."

"Then I will finish. There is not much more, only what he said to me."

"He . . . spoke to you?"

"Only at first to say, not politely, that he did not know what I was saying. So I told him: your daughter, monsieur, your daughter Kerry, Kerry Cromer, who was here on this spot, waiting for me, when you came. You see, Kerry, in a way I was right. He came, but perhaps it would have been better for Mr. Drummond to tell you the truth. Then you would have been prepared. He, too. He did not say one more word to me, but he looked strange. Moved? No. Stunned — something like that. He only repeated your name slowly, and then he said — not to me, but to himself, two or three times — he said: my God. Softly. I left him because I was afraid you would leave me behind and —"

He stopped. At the door, Benjamin Drummond was looking at them with a brow creased with worry.

"Kerry, are you all right?"

"Her father came and she ran away," said Pierre.

"You said you recognized him," Kerry said, "but —"

"Kerry, it is there for everybody to see. Everybody? No, not everybody. Not your fellow workers at the office, who are not expecting to see a resemblance. But others more observant. People who love you. And painters. When I paint your portrait, I shall have to put his eyebrows, his mouth, his forehead. Of course he is a man, and old, and you are young and soft and feminine — but you are father and daughter."

"When you came out of the water," Benjamin Drummond said, "I asked you if we'd met before. I meant it. But I didn't place the resemblance. It wasn't until I went up to see your mother that everything fell into place. I thought you ought to be told. But hell, how could I make her tell you if she didn't want to?"

"It's impossible. It's — you're all wrong," Kerry told him. "He wrote a message, and I read it. Fifteen years. It said fifteen years. It —"

"That's what it was — fifteen years," Benjamin said. "She left him to come to me, but it wasn't the first time they'd been together. It was the third. She's not an easy woman to get facts out of, but I didn't have your delicacy in shying away from her past. What I wanted to know, I found out. And of course I saw your father, not once but many times, so when I saw you —"

"And now you know the truth, Kerry, and I am glad," Pierre told her. "And now we are on the way to St. Malo and — are you listening?"

"Yes."

"You must come with me to Paris to meet my mother and my father."

"No."

258

"They must see you in the end. Why not now? There is no reason for you to go to London." He turned to Benjamin. "Tell her she must come to Paris with me."

Benjamin glanced at Kerry, but could read nothing on her face.

"Look, Kerry's aboard my yacht, hired, and I'm captain, self-appointed," he said firmly. "Therefore she's in my charge and under my jurisdiction. Any proposals or propositions will have to come through me. Is that understood?"

"Certainly. Through you," Pierre said, "I ask if she will come and stay with my parents in Paris."

"Will you, Kerry?"

"Yes."

"She'll go. As she will then not be in my charge or under my jurisdiction," Benjamin said, "I'd like to know who's going to be responsible for her."

"Naturally, I am," said Pierre. "Through you, I ask her if she will consider me in marriage."

"No," said Kerry.

"I wouldn't presume to give you advice, Kerry," Benjamin told her, "but it sounds a good idea to me. Especially as you're going to see his mother first. Once you get a look at a guy's mother, Connie says, you get to know the guy. You can't really fatten a guy up, either, unless you're married to him, and Connie says that's what you'd like to do — feed him and fill him out. And I don't know whether your father and your mother are going to have yet another get-together, but whether they do or whether they don't, my guess is that Lord Hazing will make some claim on your attention, if not your affections. He knows where to find you. So why don't you consider Pierre's proposition? Why don't you try it? I'll be there, just two blocks away, to see he treats you right, and if your father shows up, I can arrange a reunion — him and me and Pierre's father, what could be nicer? Come on, Kerry; will you try it?"

"Yes," said Kerry.

Benjamin heaved a sigh of relief.

"That's fixed, then," he said. "Now will the two of you come up aloft and get some nice, hot tea into you?"

We hope you have enjoyed this Large Print book. Other G.K. Hall & Co. or Chivers Press Large Print books are available at your library or directly from the publishers.

For more information about current and upcoming titles, please call or write, without obligation, to:

G.K. Hall & Co.
P.O. Box 159
Thorndike, Maine 04986 USA
Tel. (800) 257-5157

OR

Chivers Press Limited
Windsor Bridge Road
Bath BA2 3AX
England
Tel. (0225) 335336

All our Large Print titles are designed for easy reading, and all our books are made to last.